A Working
Arrangement

Ken Hayton

ISBN 0-9550130-0-3

Cover illustration by Gill Hayton

Prepared and printed by:
York Publishing Services Ltd
64 Hallfield Road
Layerthorpe
York YO31 7ZQ
Tel: 01904 431213; Website: www.yps-publishing.co.uk

CONTENTS

Dedication

This book is of course a work of fiction but it was inspired by an actual event. In January, 1881, the brig 'Visiter' was wrecked in Robin Hood's Bay and the dreadful North-Easterly gale made the launching of the lifeboat from Whitby quite impossible. The only course available was to haul the boat overland through snowdrifts several feet deep and launch her from the landing at Baytown. The seas were tumultuous and it required two attempts to reach the wreck, the first attempt having been beaten back when a huge wave smashed the oars and injured some of the crew. When, years ago, I first read the plaque commemorating this event on the hill running down into Baytown, I knew that some day I would have to write about it and draw public attention to what was a truly remarkable achievement.

And so I wrote my novel, which is a sort of family saga involving folk who lived, worked and died on the coastal strip between Whitby and Scarborough. The climax of the story is based upon the rescue of the 'Visiter'. Usually in a novel, the characters are all fictional but in this case the names of the principal heroes of the rescue have been retained, as a tribute to their courage and resolve. This was a tremendous undertaking, but typical of the selfless dedication which men of the R.N.L.I. have shown over the years and indeed to this very day. We who have 'gone down to the sea in ships', for whatever purpose, have been glad to know that they are ever ready to render assistance and, as a mark of my gratitude, I would like to dedicate this book to them.

Ken Hayton

AUTHORS NOTES AND ACKNOWLEDGEMENTS

Whilst my original inspiration came from reading the commemorative tablet at Robin Hood's Bay, I was able to amplify the details of the rescue from reports in the local press at that time but also, and more importantly, from the excellent little booklet 'The Visiter Rescue' published by Bayfair. I would strongly recommend this book to those seeking a more factually based account of the event.

For the rest of the tale, inspiration came from episodes in my own family history, although greatly removed in time and place from the setting of this story. It was in Cumberland in 1758 that my g.g.g.g. grandfather, Daniel Hayton, caused those moving words to be inscribed on Jane's headstone and it is his story, part documented, part conjectural and part pure invention, which is told in this novel. It is from Daniel and Ruth that I am descended.

I am indebted to Stephen Caunce for all the information he gave me about the horselads of East Yorkshire and his book, 'Amongst the Horses' has been an encyclopaedia of farming practice, which has sustained me throughout my writing. I hope he will forgive me for postulating the possibility of exporting the Wold's system to the North Yorkshire coast, where soil, weather and customs are rather different.

My thanks are very much due to my wife Gill for the design of the cover; Ann and Tony Jenkins of The Shire Horse Farm, Staintondale, have kindly provided pictures of their lovely animals to help her in its creation and assistance has also been rendered by Gavin and Jennifer Thow in this respect. I am deeply grateful to Dave Mercer of York Publishing Services who has guided me carefully through this whole process of publication. His advice has been invaluable and his cheerful encouragement has rendered the project thoroughly enjoyable.

It was nice also to receive advice and encouragement from local author, Fred Normandale. Our literary efforts are quite different but our attitudes to publishing strikingly similar!

Thanks are due to my daughter, Alison Findlay, for her valuable criticism and advice during the writing of this book. I hope she will not disown any connection with the finished product. My proofreaders, Audrey Grundy and Sara Wakelan, are to be congratulated on their patience and thoroughness in weeding out textual errors. They are fortunate in not having to be held responsible for the quality of the contents. Above all, however, it is Gill's enthusiasm and encouragement which has lead to these words actually appearing in print.

Ken Hayton
April 2005

Synopsis

A Working Arrangement is the story of one man's unyielding ambition and powerful passions. It is the story too of conflict, compromise and cooperation between man and nature culminating in an heroic battle against ferocious elements in order to save lives.

The relationship between man and woman is also one of conflict, cooperation and compromise, as is amply portrayed in the story of Daniel, Jane and Ruth. Contentment and anger, happiness and sorrow, strong physical passion and tenderness are all experienced in turn by the characters in this tale, the setting of which is the beautiful, but often harsh, countryside of the North Yorkshire coast in the mid nineteenth century.

Chapter 1

The Hireling

He felt terribly self conscious as he stood with, and yet slightly aloof from, all the other men in a loose line outside the Black Swan in Whitby. Dressed in smart moleskin breeches, clean white shirt and new blue jacket, with shiny black boots, he made quite a fine figure in the weak November sunshine. The coil of horsehair was worn in his cap with a pride borne from achievement and his partially open jacket, fastened only at the top by a short piece of chain, displayed a chest which, if not yet of the fullness to be found in a fully mature man, nonetheless demonstrated a fine physique, which was further enhanced by the long, straight limbs. This was the traditional presentation of a man seeking employment in a highly specialised branch of farming. He was a horseman, as the coil of hair proclaimed, and the display of physical stature was not simply exhibitionism but an assertion that he was capable of carrying corn. He was confident that he had the qualifications and the ability to hold down a job but he was nervous because this was the first time he had tried to sell his labour in the open market. But circumstances had obliged him to do so and here he was at the Martinmas hiring, already experiencing a strong feeling of distaste at the necessity of being examined, albeit from afar, like a piece of meat on a butcher's slab. The examining body was of course the farmers who were gathered across the street in small knots, exchanging greetings and news but also eyeing up the candidates, sounding out their neighbours on the level of wages to be offered and seeking information about unfamiliar faces in the labour market. Newcomers such as himself would be discussed and conjectured over before an exploratory move was made. He reminded himself to maintain a pleasant expression and hide the bitterness he felt at now being forced to negotiate for his living. He very nearly succeeded.

Across the street Richard Farlam was talking with his foreman George Buckram and discussing that very point.

"Yes sir, I kin see 'e's got t' shape for't job and looks bright enough but 'e looks fair miserable. We disn't want no trouble makers amongst t'lads."

"True George," replied Farlam,
"But I like the look of him so have a word will you?"

George strolled across and going directly up to the young man greeted him with

"Noo m'lad. Dost'a want hiring then?"

"Aye, ah do."

"As a horse lad ah see."

"As a waggoner" he was corrected.

George was surprised and amused. "Tha looks a bit young for't job. 'Ave you 'ad much experience?"

"Aye, ah 'ave" was the confident reply.

"Well tha looks strong enough to carry but can ya stack an' thack?"

"Yes ah can." answered Daniel equally confidently and with pride because the ability to stack and thatch was highly prized by employers. George smiled and shook his head.

"My word but yer last boss must be desperate sad to see thee go; 'ow could he bear to part with thee?"

The bitterness broke out then beyond disguise.

"'E hed no choice mister. It was me father as a've allus worked for but 'e's 'ad 'is farm taken from 'im."

Comprehension dawned upon George Buckram.

"Wye now you must be one of John Robinson's boys, let me see, Daniel is it?", and when he received a nod of assent he continued

"Aye, well we all heard about that an' ahm sure we are all very sorry 'bout it. But I suppose it was business."

"Oh aye, it was business all right. 'Is Lordship wanted t'land and that was that."

There was certainly no disguising the bitterness now.

His Lordship had indeed wanted the land quite badly. High Stoupe farm was adjacent to the huge alum works where the company had been experiencing diminishing returns owing to the deterioration of the alum bearing shale as they worked it westwards. The main seams, the richest in terms of alum content, dipped down to the north and ran immediately through and below the land of High Stoupe. His Lordship had been offered a sum of money for this land which he could not afford to refuse so that, when the tenancy period expired on St Michaelmas last, John Robinson was told that it would not be renewed. Local wisdom was that the investors had made fools of themselves and that alum mining was a dying trade. They were to be proved right within a couple of years but this was no solace to the Robinsons. His Lordship, to give him his due, had done something for the dispossessed family. Daniel's mother, Mary, and his sister, Naomi, were found places as servants at the Castle, whilst his father was employed at the home farm. There were however no places for Daniel and his younger brother, Tom, who had volunteered for the Royal Navy and was now away serving at sea. They had not heard from him for some time. Daniel had found a temporary job as casual labourer, with no special responsibilities and no prospects, so here he was some four weeks later trying to improve his situation. Meanwhile the fields and pastures of High Stoupe were even now being torn up and the empty buildings, Daniel's home for all the sixteen years of his life, were adapted for use in the alum works. Or so he had heard. He could not bear to go and see for himself.

"Well noo", continued George "we are needin' a horseman or two this year so we can maybe offer thee a job."

"As waggoner?" Daniel asked.

"Nay lad, tha can't expect a job as boss of eight or nine lads, some older and with more experience than thee! No we 'ave a waggoner, a good un an' all, and we 'ave a good thirdy too." He looked again at Daniel appraisingly. "Mebbe we could mak thee a fourther, aye I think we might, so 'ow about that?"

It was well below the position which Daniel had wished for but reason told him that this sounded to be a large farm and probably had better prospects for him.

"Aye all right then but ah'll be wantin' £15".

George laughed outright. "That's more than our waggoner gets. Ye can 'ave 12 and all found."

"All found! Well I should hope so" said Daniel "but ah must have at least 14."

The haggling continued until Daniel had stuck fast at £13 and a 'fest' of £1.

"Well, ah shall 'ave to ask Mr Farlam about that" said George. "Just you wait there." And with that he crossed the street to consult with the tall and immaculately dressed gentleman who had been watching this by-play intently. That was when Daniel learned that his prospective employer was

Mr Richard Farlam, owner of Highfield Hall and its large farm, the biggest indeed in the whole area save for his Lordship's estates. He had heard of Farlam; indeed who hadn't in this part of the world? There were reckoned to be about forty or fifty horses in his stables, all beautiful, pure bred, Clydesdales. Most of what he had heard about the man himself had been good too; a stern master but fair; not too generous with the money but the living conditions were good. Daniel was beginning to regret holding out for so much money and risking losing the job but he couldn't back down now. He squared his shoulders and awaited the outcome of the conference.

It was George who was now the firm advocate for the lad. He had been impressed with his spirit and the qualifications which he claimed to have. He looked strong enough and they needed men who could stack the corn and hay, thatching it against the weather. But Mr Farlam, who had been the one to instigate the contact, was now playing devil's advocate.

"A bit young George, to have so many lads under him. Why one or two will be quite a deal older than he."

"He'll brook no nonsense Mr Farlam." replied George. "Yon's a lad who has ambition and authority. 'E's 'ad experience of responsibility even if t'were on a small farm."

"Yes but £13 George?"

"Aye that's what 'e asks sir"; he paused and grinned "But on'y a pund fest!"

Farlam conceded with a nod. "All right then George, I'll back your judgement; I'll go and introduce myself."

Daniel's hopes rose as Mr Farlam crossed the street towards him; clearly he had not been rejected out of hand. He was to be even more heartened by the opening remarks.

"Well now, Mr Robinson, I know your father and of his recent troubles and I know of his reputation for hard work so I'm thinking you'll not be letting him down if I offer you a job."

"No sir, nor you either." replied Daniel, pleased by the salutation and the kindly words.

"You're a hard bargainer and I shall be wanting my money's worth." The smile belied the sharp words and Mr Farlam extended his hand. "£13 pounds then?"

Daniel hesitated until Farlam continued, "Oh yes and £1 fastening penny." A handshake and the handing over of £1 completed the bargain and Daniel was now bound for a twelvemonth at Highfield Farm. Perhaps things were not so bad after all. Yes, it was true that he had lost his home and his position of trust and responsibility with his father but there was another side to the situation. He was now independent. True he would be without his father's support and he had to stand alone and win the respect of his new work mates and employer but he was confident that he could do that.

* * * * *

There were two days before he had to take up his new job and back at the cottage by the Home farm he was made a fuss of by the family in the time before he left. They were much impressed by his achievement in being given a job at Highfield. John Robinson had many good words to say about the farm and his new employer.

"Aye a grand big farm, Highfield and a real gentleman, Mr Farlam, a widower. Came over from East Riding way about fifteen year ago with just his daughter, a little girl then, with an older woman, who was a sort of nursemaid, and George Buckram who had been his foreman. Decent fella' George, and he quickly took up with a lass from Bay Town, Alice Jenson, a deal younger than him but they seemed well suited.

Got married quickly enough anyway. I think they have but one lass at present."

"Aye and that's all there's likely to be from what I hear." said Mary Robinson quietly and a little sadly.

"Any road at all" continued John, "they hadn't been there above eighteen months and Farlam had built himself a grand new Hall. He and his little lass moved into that but left the old farmhouse for George and Alice and ever since they have been working as hinds to look after the horse lads. But the horses, Daniel! Those horses! If you think we've had some good 'uns wait till you clap eyes on his stable. Wonderful Clydesdales, always well turned out and it will be a proud day for me when I see's you bringing his smart rig into town."

"You'll be living in with the Buckrams, Daniel" commented his mother. "It's Alice Buckram who really acts as hind and they say she runs a good house."

"Aye", John Robinson agreed, "They say as 'ow t'is a good meat house."

Daniel smiled for he enjoyed his food as much as any healthy young man.

Mrs Robinson sniffed disparagingly, "Meat or no meat he'll be well cared for and kept clean and warm. She's a decent little body, Alice Buckram, even if she is not fortunate with her health."

Daniel had to endure the usual instructions from his parents as to how to behave himself. From his mother it was mainly a matter of looking after himself, being polite and expressing appreciation for his accommodation and boarding; from his father it was more a question of how to conduct himself with his working mates; how to show the proper respect for his superiors in the complicated farm hierarchy but also how to exercise the proper authority over his underlings.

John explained to his son that Richard Farlam had imported from the Wolds, not only his foreman and blood stock, but also the traditional East Riding practices in labour management. This had been a source of amusement and mystification to the local populace but they had gradually come to acknowledge that it worked well, although several years later few were yet fully conversant with the nomenclature and pecking order. The top horseman, responsible for all the horse lads, their turnouts and discipline in the field, was called the waggoner. He in turn came under the ultimate authority of the foreman, which meant that the second ranked horse lad was known as a 'thirdy'. Then came the 'fourther' and so on down the line to the youngest and smallest of the young boys, who was somewhat whimsically referred to as the 'least lad'. He, like the other young boys however, did his share of the work of mucking out, cleaning the collars and martingales. maintaining the harness in good order and polishing the brasses for when the animals appeared in public. The foreman was also in charge of all the other workers on the farm, from ordinary labourers to shepherd and beastman and including the grooms who attended the riding horses and breeding stock. His was a job of immense and wide ranging responsibility on such a large farm and as such it was right that he commanded great respect. This was most nearly the sort of advice Daniel wanted to hear for he was determined to start off right. It was, after all, to be his living for the foreseeable future and it commenced on Monday. It was still very dark, well before dawn in fact when he set off from the Home farm on that Monday morning to walk the eight miles to Highfield. His pack contained two changes of working clothes, against the drenchings he could expect, his carefully wrapped best clothes and a few personal bits and bobs. Packed on top was one of his mother's nice bramble and apple pies but this was not for his own use; it was a present to Alice Buckram. Mary Robinson was not above a little bribery to ensure that her son was well looked after.

* * * * *

It was bitterly cold outside and, to be frank, not much better inside the huge old farmhouse. Inside the attics, where the lads slept, it was not unusual to find a thick layer of frost on the walls after a particularly hard night. Not that this night had produced a very keen frost. It was the wind that made the difference. A piercing northeaster, which came whistling across the sea and was now knifing through all but the thickest garments. They were astir now, George could hear, and about time too. Because it was so dark these mornings, he had altered the routine to allow them to sleep in till 6:00 a.m., a good hour later than in the summertime. There was still time to get the horses mucked out, fed and groomed, for them to have their breakfasts and then to get the teams out on the fields for first light at about 7:30 a.m. There'd be a good breakfast for them this morning as well, a hot one in deference to the wintry weather. A bowl of milk of course but hot boiled bacon too; George felt his appetite rising as he smelt the meat which Alice was heating up in the copper. They tumbled downstairs and after a brief 'good morning' went out into the stables. George knew that he didn't need to follow. Harry was as good a waggoner as he had known in his extensive experience on the land and he could be relied upon to see that everything was done properly. Nonetheless he couldn't resist the temptation to wander in after a half hour or so, ostensibly to have a chat about the work in hand but also to keep an eye on how things were going. It was actually much warmer in the stables than the house because of the body heat generated by the horses. He watched in approval as the business of feeding was undertaken. This was the waggoner's overall responsibility and he measured out the oats, about half a stone for each horse at this time of day. There was hay in the mangers too but this was not needed so much if the quantity of oats was sufficient. George caught a small movement out of the corner of his eye and smiled as he recognised that Daniel Robinson was slipping a bit of linseed cake into his horses feed. Good for the coat and spirits of the horse but expensive and it had doubtless been filched from the beastman's supplies. He pretended that he hadn't seen, for there was no way that he would discipline Daniel for his action; he had done it himself too often as a lad, trying hard to preserve the well-being and appearance of his horses. The lads looked and sounded cheerful enough. Time for a word with Harry about the ploughing to be done today. It was vital that they get as much done as possible. Heavy rainfall in October followed by some snow in November had held up the job and now the cold, dry spell must be taken advantage of before the hard frosts really did set in and the ground became too hard. There was much high spirited and lively conversation at breakfast, another indication that all was well with his labour force. George considered himself lucky that he had such a well balanced crew. He himself, as foreman, was of course the number one man but Harry, second in the hierarchy and an employee at Highfield for several years, was the lynch pin, a truly good waggoner who knew his job thoroughly and commanded the respect of his underlings. A pity he would be leaving at the end of next year but he was to be married and the exigencies of the job of horseman demanded that only single lads, who could live in, were employable. Dick Chapman, the 'thirdy' now in his second year at the farm, was big and beefy, competent and hard working but inclined to surliness. More jealous than most of his position in the ranking status, he seemed to resent the trust and reliance now being reposed upon the shoulders of the 'fourther' immediately below him. Now there was a good find, George thought with satisfaction. Young Daniel Robinson was fitting in well and more than pulling his weight within the three weeks that he had been at Highfield.. All the claims he had made at the hirings had been justified. He could certainly handle his horses well, cared for them properly and showed signs of becoming an excellent ploughman. The strength and stamina he had already shown boded well for his ability to handle the exhausting work of the harvesting in the summer to come. He was a pleasant enough lad too, although of few words and a rather serious disposition. His quietly assured manner gave him an easy ascendancy over his subordinates, despite the fact that both were a little older than he. The only reservation which George had was that he was occasionally unable to conceal the bitterness occasioned by the loss of the parental farm. It was manifested in an antipathy to and distrust of landowners in general, including, to George's irritation, his own employer, Mr Farlam, a man who George thought to be the best employer in the district. Surely the lad would come to realise how lucky he was in due course. Of the others, Burt, amiable and not too intellectually well endowed, was a natural born follower, all too ready to stand down in favour of someone else's opinion. The only reason that he was ranked higher than the very much brighter Jed was the latter's inclination to silliness and lack of responsibility. All in all they had blended into an efficient, easily run unit. Characteristically, George gave himself no credit for his careful management of these young people. He smiled a lot but took little part in the conversation and was ready at the right moment to order an end to the meal and a start on the day's work in the fields.

As foreman, George had many other duties than merely overseeing the work and welfare of the horse lads. Indeed, after discussing the ploughing schedule with Harry, he had to have a word with Abel the shepherd and Nick the beastman. Those two were competing for pasture now that the winter weather was likely to drive the sheep down from the moors. The cattle must be moved into their winter byres although the sheep, hardy Swaledale crosses, remained outdoors all winter. There was the horse breeding element too and, although he usually deferred to the opinions of his employer Mr Farlam, who was after all an acknowledged expert in the field when it came to the breeding programme, George nonetheless had the overall responsibility for the welfare of the blood-stock and management of the grooms.

The farm was indeed very large and traditionally mixed in its production of cereal crops, root crops, beef and mutton but the breeding of draught horses was, for this region of Yorkshire, an unusually large part of the farm activity. With all these multifarious responsibilities George was a very busy man and laboured long and hard, turning his hand to work wherever it was needed. But then all the Buckram family were kept busy. Alice, working as hind to the living in horse lads, was also involved in the production of the dairy products and a delightful spin off for the boys was the plentiful supply of farm butter, milk and occasionally cream. Apart from her domestic duties, she could be called upon to work in the fields along with the farm labourers especially at hay and harvest time when many other women were temporarily recruited from the surrounding villages. Like so many of her kind, this amiable and contented woman went quietly about her work making no ripples on the ordered surface of the farm routine and taking none of the limelight during the times of success or trouble. Her contribution to the smooth running of this community was largely undervalued precisely because it was a smooth running community. Only when she was missing was there an appreciation of her indispensability and that happened seldom if ever.

Even little Ruth played her part in the family fortunes. As soon as she was old enough she was relied upon to let out and feed the hens, collect the eggs, help bring in the cattle for milking and mix the food for the calves. She did all this before trudging off to school in the village with her little packet of bread and cheese with the occasional small pastry treat which her mother had prepared. The sheep dogs were Abel's responsibility and she was not allowed to feed them or fondle them in any way. She was ten years old now and on a Sunday after church, she often walked down into Bay Town and helped with the baiting of pots in summer and lines in winter for her uncle Jethro Jenson. The work was perhaps repetitive and boring but care had to be taken not to impale one's fingers on the hooks or sepsis would often set in with painful and sometimes dire results. On the plus side there was always a jolly atmosphere in the baiting shed. Uncle Jethro and her cousin Simeon kept up a continuous banter whilst cousin Jessica was a mine of delicious gossip and information as to the 'doings' in the town. After work was finished there would be a stroll up King Street and then along The Bolts to her uncle and aunt's cosy little cottage where there might be fish pie or delicious crab sandwiches for tea. Older than Ruth by some five years, Jessica was good looking enough to attract the attention of all the boys and a good number of older men too. Ruth had noticed that her uncle Jethro and aunt Maria were not only aware of this but were somehow worried about it at times. Ruth couldn't see what it was that they might be concerned about for Jessica was always accompanied and helped by her male friends whenever she went out. Ruth would occasionally go mussel and flither collecting with Jessica and there was always at least one young man who tagged along to help with carrying the bass bags. These expeditions were fun but Ruth frequently found that the attentions of her cousin would be monopolised by her male consort whilst she was consigned to seeking mussel beds far away from the headquarters of the gathering party. When she returned there would sometimes be no sign of mussel collecting going on; rather would they be resting on the sands in a very companionable fashion.

* * * * *

Daniel eased his team out into the lane behind Dick Chapman thus preserving the order of seniority in the ploughing force. They were filing past the Old Hall and Mr Farlam himself was watching their progress as they made for the big south pasture, which was destined for a crop of swedes this year. He inspected each horse critically as it passed and acknowledged each 'morning sir' with a nod and a smile for each horse was well turned out with gleaming coat and a neatly bobbed tail. The lads themselves looked a sorry sight in comparison, wearing as they did a motley collection of old clothes designed to keep out the weather rather than make a fashion statement. George was standing with Mr Farlam and smiled appreciatively as the twelve beautiful horses plodded by; the lads were doing him proud. Glancing back Daniel saw a young woman leading from the Hall stable a magnificent hunter, which she mounted with the aid of a groom. It was Jane Farlam and he had noted before how well she rode. Stopping at the group by the gate, she exchanged a few words with the two men and then, as George touched his battered old hat, she trotted off down the road towards Whitby.

"Not for the likes of you, me lad" sneered Dick Chapman, who had been following Daniel's gaze.

Daniel felt no need to reply to this remark and held his tongue, usually the best policy when Dick seemed bent on goading him, but the 'thirdy' pressed on with "Member of the gentry that lady; wouldn't want to look at a miserable workin' lad on hard times now would she, even if you was half way decent lookin'."

Nettled, because his interest had been purely in the lovely horse and the way it was being ridden, Daniel retained his composure and replied quietly with a smile "Wye then Dick, I'd best step down in favour of you eh? She wouldn't stand a chance then, would she?"

This evoked a cackle of laughter from Jed for Chapman's decided lack of success in the field of romantic endeavour had been the subject of much good-natured leg pulling at supper last night. The joke had evidently worn thin for the older lad and a crease of irritation appeared on his brow.

"Keep your place in line Burt" he shouted. "What are you thinkin' of fourther; keep them teams behind you well up."

Looking worried, Burt urged his team forward to make up the few yards he had fallen behind but nobody else took the reprimand seriously and they continued in silence until they reached the plough land.

Daniel brought his team into the field, hitched up the plough and awaited the signal to begin from the 'wag'. Once again there was a strict code of precedence and he fell in behind the 'thirdy' striving hard to maintain the beautifully precise furrowing of the field. Any shoddy work would be bitterly criticised he knew but it was not just for his own pride and satisfaction that he tried so hard to produce a good result; there was the collective pride of the whole group of Highfield horsemen to consider. Visitors, including workers from neighbouring farms taking a Sunday afternoon stroll, would cast an eye over the fields and quickly note the standard of the ploughing. Highfield had a reputation to maintain for at the last ploughing match in the area Harry had walked away with the champion's trophy with Dick also well placed in the final results. Daniel, who had prided himself on his ability to handle horses well and especially to the plough, was forced to admit that he still had much to learn. He was more than willing to do so and hung upon the words of his 'wag' for scraps of knowledge and even endured the sarcasm of the misanthropic Dick Chapman to pick up some of the tricks of the trade. All in all he was satisfied with his progress at fitting into the establishment at the farm. He had managed to impress his authority over his two subordinates without difficulty, he seemed to have made a good start with the foreman and waggoner and he had made an uneasy truce between himself and the 'thirdy'. That in fact was his only worry. It had proved to be enormously difficult to achieve even that poor relationship with Dick Chapman and Daniel could not understand where he had gone wrong. The answer of course was in the latter's basic insecurity, which was something that Daniel could not appreciate. If he had been aware of the high regard in which he was held by both George and Harry, a fact which had been registered by all the other lads, then he might have understood something of the reason for this latent ill-feeling. As for the work, he was in his element. He had always loved the horses on his father's farm and liked nothing better than to be working with them. He had learnt a good deal from John Robinson, himself a very good horseman, and now he was in charge of four of the finest specimens of shire horses he had ever seen. They were the elite because they had been bred on the farm from the fine animals which it housed. At least a half of the horses on the farm were used for breeding purposes and sold on to farmers across the whole of the north of England, who appreciated the fine qualities of the blood-stock. The breeding mares and riding horses were in the charge of special grooms who had nothing to do with the general running of the farm and formed a separate community of their own. Daniel thought himself very fortunate to have in his charge four of these beautiful animals. He was lucky too in their temperaments; Bonny, Blossom and Biddy were gentle, willing creatures who responded well to kindness and attention; Bess was a bit of a handful, slightly wilful and lazy, but manageable for all that. He quickly established a good rapport with them all and was learning about their individual quirks and strengths. Chip, his boy, did his share of the grooming and most of the mucking out but Daniel insisted upon doing the feeding himself after Harry had measured out the supply of oats. As a worker he had shown himself to be competent, hard working and willing to learn. His relationship with the rest of the crew was fine; regarded as quiet and just a little reserved, he was nonetheless amicable enough and they remained unaware of the resentment and bitterness which George had detected and discussed with Mr Farlam. His position therefore seemed secure and furthermore a happy one. It was only deep within the boy that the anger remained and the determination to rise above his current station never diminished.

Something of this disposition emerged at Christmas time when, after the service in the little chapel at the castle, he spoke with his father about the prospects of the whole family. He was upset because John seemed to have accepted his new lot as a hired labourer when once he had been master of his own farm. The cramped conditions of the tiny tied cottage accentuated the difference in lifestyle which had affected them all. Although it was difficult for Daniel to believe, all the evidence pointed to the fact that John had lost ambition with the loss of the land he had farmed for more than eighteen years. He simply felt too old and dispirited to start again and was reluctant to embark upon another venture which might lead to failure when security now seemed to be assured. Daniel was not so sure about the security aspect. If his Lordship chose, he argued, the Robinsons could also be evicted from the cottage and new labourers taken on at the next hirings. He was clearly not inclined to accept the landlord's word to the contrary. John smiled encouragingly when his son expressed his intention to run his own farm just as soon as he could, progressing through the post of foreman on a large farm before taking the plunge.

"Best of all father is to own your own land" he said passionately. "Your land to hold and farm as you please, with no landlord to be beholden to, no way that you can be turned off. That's what I want; that's what I shall have one day!"

John smiled indulgently and wished his son well in his ambition, not wanting to deflate the moment of enthusiasm by asking how this would be achieved. And yet he detected in Daniel's manner a change of character since their eviction from High Stoupe. Where there had been a quiet but sunny individual, content with his life on the farm there was now a fierce determination and a hardness which had not been there before. He worried about that hardness just a little.

The conversation turned to technical matters and John wanted to know how the work was going and what the conditions were like. He listened in approval as Daniel told him that in an effort to make up the time lost through the weather, no less than eight teams had been working at one time, with George Buckram leading one of them, but now they had managed to turn over all but a few acres and that should be completed before the hard frosts set in. Daniel waxed lyrical over his horses.

"By God but you were right father." he exclaimed. "I'd never seen such beauties before and there's over fifty head of them on the farm, half of them in use as breeding stock. Mind, that's including the riding horses of course."

He told of his own four charges and how he looked after them, receiving a few tips from the older man, and the talk turned to the implements and how the new strong but lightweight ploughs, which Mr Farlam had bought, meant that two horses could now do the work of the three which would have been necessary to pull the old ploughs he had been used to. Mrs Robinson wanted to hear all about his accommodation and the fare he received. She seemed to be well pleased with his description of the conditions and treatment.

"I don't know how that little body copes with all you great big lads. Does she have no help?"

Daniel told her that the young daughter, Ruth, shared a good deal of the housework even though she was only ten and they seemed to manage just fine. The rest of the family wanted to know about the people he lived and worked with and he gave some amusing but unflattering descriptions of Burt, Dick and Jed. He praised George and Harry, expressing his admiration for their knowledge of horses and farming practice and his appreciation of their firm but fair leadership. Mr Farlam, he was forced to admit when pressed, was a decent enough chap for a landowner and, when he incautiously mentioned the daughter Jane, who rode so well, eyebrows went up and he was subjected to a good deal of ribbing about marrying the boss's daughter as a sure way of getting on in life. The vehemence of his denial of there being any such thoughts in his head only added to the humour of the situation and provoked more laughter from his sister Naomi; his parents did however exchange a quick glance amidst all the merriment. Even brought up as he had been on their fairly remote farm and kept busy as he was by the unremitting toil associated with that life, there had been nonetheless plenty of opportunities for Daniel to mix with other young people including several local girls. That he had apparently taken no notice of the latter was a matter which had concerned his father, who had felt it as an affront to his own manhood that he had seemingly fathered a son with no interest in the opposite sex. It just wasn't natural especially at his age of dawning knowledge and curiosity and it certainly wasn't the norm in John's experience. Only look at Sid Bateman's young lad, Curly. Just turned sixteen and was said to have fathered a child over Sleights way. In fact there was going to be a wedding – the lass's parents were seeing to that! So what was wrong with Daniel? A grand, well set up young man, of whom any father could be proud, were it not for this strange lack of interest in the opposite sex. John had chewed over this matter for some time before tentatively, and with much beating about the bush, he confided in his wife. Mary had quickly divined the depths of his worry and made haste to settle his worst fears, unspoken though they may have been.

"Nay John, there's nowt wrong with our Daniel" she said firmly. "Except mebbe' he's inherited a bit too much of his father's character."

Shocked, her husband merely stared at her in mute disbelief.

"Aye. that's right" she continued steadily "He has your pride John, and mebbe' even more so then your'n. And he is a bit shy like with the girls too. Now put those two together and you have your answer. I should think he once or twice wanted to make a move but was just too frightened of being turned down. He couldn't stand the thought of being rejected; that would have hurt his pride no end."

As John digested these words she continued soothingly, "It'll pass soon enough as he gets older and more confident. Some lass 'll likely come along and sweep him right off his feet. He's a good enough catch is our Daniel." And that too had been said with more than a touch of pride.

John had been grateful for his wife's insight and having studied his son more sympathetically since then he had come to acknowledge the truth of her argument so that now, with that interchange of glances there was also a hint of an understanding smile. Despite the cramped little cottage, or perhaps because of it, Christmas had been a convivial family reunion, a happy time with only the absence of his sailor brother as a small disappointment and Daniel felt a wrench as he made to return to Highfield. But before leaving he had looked around the sitting room taking in the simple furniture, the 'clippie' rag rugs on the floor, the shining horse brasses fixed to the beam, the china dogs on the mantelpiece and the print of the Queen on the wall. It was a homely enough scene but it struck him that there was not much to show for nearly a lifetime's work. I can do better than this he told himself. Well, this is a new year coming and I shall need to get on with the job of trying to better myself.

CHAPTER 2

THE THIRDY

It was a day such as would be fit for any artist's brush, a day when the world was at its best, when the sun shone from an unblemished blue sky and not a trace of haze spoilt the clarity of the view over the fields to the sea; a sea for once blue rather than grey or green. A day when the skylarks maintained a steady chorus from above, so high that they were visible only as tiny black dots and the lack of wind meant that the sweet scent of the drying hay suffused the surrounding atmosphere and combining with the warmth produced an incredibly soporific effect. Indeed an onlooker might have been excused for imagining that he had happened upon a scene from a fairy tale with the recumbent forms on the newly shorn grass frozen into immobility by some magic spell. Only a few minutes earlier and that same onlooker would have witnessed a lively enough scene as the crowd of haymakers tucked in to their lunchtime break with the usual clamour and backchat associated with leisure time, when workers got together with the women. But then the lively chatter had gradually subsided as the company laid back and simply enjoyed the blessed warmth and the comfort of a full stomach, producing the tableau described earlier. Daniel had actually dosed off when the spell was broken by the low but insistent call of their foreman. The day was passing he told them; it was essential to get on with the task in hand and of course everyone knew that that old saw of 'making hay while the sun shone' applied most particularly to their part of the world so there was little grumbling at being recalled to their labours after so short a spell of rest. Speed was the great priority during haytime, especially on the North Yorkshire coast with its potential for inclement conditions, even in midsummer. The farmer lucky enough to have cut at the right time and found a sunny spell to dry his hay was desperate to bring it in, once it was adjudged ready for stacking and before a summer storm came along to ruin the crop. Mr Farlam's hay crop had lain in almost uninterrupted sunshine for several days, had been turned regularly and was now absolutely right for bringing in. Consequently all the regular farm workers, horsemen and labourers alike, were on duty as well as all the casual labour from the surrounding area which could be assembled for the day and this included many of their womenfolk. The numbers of women had been recently augmented. Across the field had come a party of females bearing the traditional midday meal. The smiling scullery maid, the dimpled cook and the demure chambermaid, all from Highfield Hall, were clearly enjoying the prospect of the picnic, the novelty of the occasion mitigating the labour of lugging the heavy baskets across to the workers. Looking up from his work, Daniel had been surprised to see Miss Farlam who, with Alice Buckram, was carrying a huge wicker hamper. She wore a colourful cotton dress which swayed as she walked in the cramped style necessitated by coping with the weight of the huge basket, her left hip and breast thrust out in a compensatory balancing pose and with a ridiculously large sun hat perched on her golden curls. She was obviously enjoying the occasion as much as everyone else. With his reservations about the landed classes, Daniel was once again compelled to acknowledge the easy relationship she had with the group of workers, and indeed they with her, as she exchanged banter with them and helped to hand out the food and pour the tea from one of the four large tin containers which young Ruth and the chambermaid had carried, a handle in each hand. Highfield farm, like many others, was now providing tea for its workers upon special occasions such as this. Formerly the precious leaves would have remained locked up in an elaborate caddy in the dining room of the Hall and its dispensation to the labourers never considered as a possibility but, what with the reduction in tax and the fact that the East India Company no longer held the monopoly on tea, prices had been tumbling for several years now and it had been adopted by many in the working classes as a regular drink. At first Daniel was not sure that he liked this beverage but he accepted it and found it to be very thirst quenching; it was better than beer in this respect he thought. The food he found to be simple but delicious. There was bread and cheese of course, the staple diet of the farm hands but also cakes which had been made by Alice Buckram to her own special recipe. They were a brilliant yellow in colour and Daniel had found that this was characteristic of baking with the eggs of hens fed on Indian corn, which was the practice at Highfield farm. All the yolks were of a similar bright colour and they imparted this to every dish in which they partook. Whether this affected the taste Daniel didn't know but he was sure he had never tasted anything so wonderful as Alice Buckram's cakes. Wisely he had refrained from extolling the virtues of this accomplishment on his trips home. Whilst happy that her son was being well provided for, Mary Robinson was sufficiently proud of her culinary ability as to take a dim view of unfavourable comparisons with another woman's work!

Daniel trudged back to the stack yard. The business of bringing the cart loads of hay in was deputed to the lads and the older men were engaged in the job of building the stacks. Daniel's accomplishment in this task, of which he had boasted at the hirings, was now put to the test and George was pleased to see that he lived up to his promise, distributing the hay neatly and with skill so that the stack rose in perfect symmetry and with homogenous composition. Work proceeded steadily and swiftly, the men concentrating hard upon their individual roles, as cartload after cartload of hay was brought in and Daniel was hardly aware of the procession of womenfolk returning with the empty baskets and standing to watch for a while as the stack grew in size. It was hard work of course and it became harder, as the level of the stack rose and hay had to be forked high into the air to be received by the stackers, but there was a rhythm to it all as the men worked with great cohesion and with great speed. It was as well that they did so. Unnoticed by all but George and a few of the older hands, a certain hardness had appeared in the blue of the sky. If anything it was getting hotter and had become very close and humid; there was not a breath of wind to relieve this. George kept glancing suspiciously around and noticed that the western sky was darkening. There was going to be a storm. Hopefully it would not strike for a while and the crop was nearly all gathered in now. George prayed that they would finish in time and in fact they did so but with little to spare. The sky was a deep black as the last cartload arrived at the stack and the first rumbles of thunder were heard from afar. The rumbles continued apace and were now accompanied by flashes which lit up the distant western horizon. Suddenly a dazzling flash appeared from what seemed to be almost above them and it was accompanied by a tremendous crash of thunder. One horse shied and was in danger of running off in a panic but was controlled well by the lad in charge and quieted. Now came the rain and it did so in torrential sheets, driven by the wind which had also appeared as though from nowhere. Stoically the men handled the last few forkfuls of hay and the tying down was commenced, with cloths to act as temporary covers until the thatching could be done properly. It took all of them there to manage this final task in the face of a wind which mindlessly hampered their every effort and frustrated their attempts to make a neat job. George was pragmatic about this latter. "Make it fast, lads" he shouted above the din of the wind.

"Just see that she's tied down hard and we'll make a proper tidy job when its blown out." And so they did; but Daniel was put in mind of the constant battle with the weather which must exist on board the sailing ships when men wrestled with unwieldy canvas in the teeth of gales such as this but without the advantage of being able to stand on the stable, unmoving earth. He wondered how his brother was faring and wondered who was the better off of the two. He reckoned it was himself.

That night he made use gratefully of a bucket of hot water from the copper, scrubbing and soaping away the accumulated dust and dried grass which had penetrated through his clothes. Those clothes, along with those of his work mates, were even now drying out in the kitchen in front of a fire lit specially for this purpose. As he towelled himself vigorously down, a picture of Jane Farlam came into his mind, her dress swaying around her hips and the outline of her breast vivid against the blue sky. Angrily he dismissed the vision and concentrated upon the pleasure of donning a warm and dry shirt, which did not have any maddeningly irritating bits of hay sticking in its fabric. It was Sunday tomorrow but there would be no rest until the stacks had been properly thatched and protected against the weather. Doubtless there would be more annoyingly intrusive bits of hay to deal with when that was completed. The thatching of the stacks was indeed completed on the Sunday and a handful of interested spectators watched as the skilful task was undertaken. Once again George congratulated himself upon his choice of hands and in particular young Daniel, who showed himself more than equal to the job. He exchanged a glance with Mr Farlam, who had strolled down to watch the operation and they smiled appreciatively at the enthusiasm and energy of the young lad who was clearly enjoying what he was doing.

But not everyone was interested in the activity in the stack yard. Ruth, after an early dinner, was on her way down to Bay Town and her regular attendance at the baiting shed of her uncle. It was another fine day but the storm had left things clearer and fresher. Ruth always enjoyed the walk down the steep and narrow street to the dock and the spectacle of the sun glinting on the sea. Today however that sea was pounding up between the scaurs, the waves sweeping past the oak posts marking the entrance to the landing, breaking noisily and running up towards the slipway. There was only just enough room for her to slip round the sea wall and make her way to the baiting shed at the foot of Cow Field. She was greeted warmly by the family who were all engaged in preparations for the fishing on the morrow. The principal activity was the baiting of the crab pots which were standing in rows outside the door and which would be shot in the morning providing the sea moderated. Jethro seemed to think that it would. He, however, was engaged in a different task. A large salmon had been spotted earlier in the week and so the nets had been rolled out and were being inspected for damage. Part of the mesh had in fact been torn and so Jethro settled down to some mending. Ruth was fascinated by the dexterity of his fingers which, hardened and callused by the constant work and immersion in salt water as they were, deftly manipulated the twine as the repairs were effected. Conversation was as usual cheerful and lively. Today it was Jessica who was the butt of much of the humour. She was being teased about her rich and handsome new gentleman friend and, despite protestations of a lack of real interest on her part, was being asked how she would adjust to married life in a smart house up-bank. Simeon gravely advised Ruth to take a good look at her cousin for the time would soon come when she would be too grand to associate with her family and would not deign to leave the parlours of the elite at the top of the hill. When Ruth enquired as to who this paragon might be it was Jessica who snapped

"It's Jonathon Stormson they are talking about and I can tell you that he's nobbut a fancy dressed weaklin' an' he means nowt to me"

Simeon laughed and replied "Aye, but a lad wi' a good deal of brass. Tha could do a lot worse sis. Now, if I could just marry 'is Lordship's daughter tha'd be able to visit us for tea at t'castle of a Sunday."

When the mirth had subsided, Jethro said quietly "Aye he'll not be short of a guinea or two but I'd wager that he would swap it all to have his parents back."

There was a general nodding of heads in agreement and Ruth recalled that this was the son of a master mariner who had taken his wife on a voyage down to London, when their ship was sunk in a fierce storm. They had both perished leaving Jonathon to be brought up by his maiden aunt. It was rumoured that despite his sad history at the hands of the sea the boy was seeking to emulate his father and obtain a master's certificate. There was more leg pulling as Simeon warned his sister that she would have to be prepared to reconstitute the Stormson dynasty with a few spares in case of accidents.

"If that's all you can talk about, me and Ruth are goin' off for a walk" Jessica said and grabbing her cousin's hand she made for the door.

"Nay lass," said her father, "Better not take Ruth wi' thee or he might switch his affections an' then where would you be?"

Giggling despite herself Jessica pulled Ruth out through the door and they made off up into the field where the obvious questions were asked. Ruth learned that after a chance encounter, when the young man had retrieved her bonnet swept away in a fresh breeze, he had clearly been responsible for several more 'chance' encounters and had struck up conversation with Jessica culminating in an invitation to take a walk one evening along the cliffs.

"Aye, he's a good looker is Jonathon, I'll say that, but he's not the chap for me. Too posh and delicate, wi' no idea 'ow to treat a girl on a nice night on't cliff tops. I mean 'slow' is too fast a word for 'im; in fact I reckon as 'ow he doesn't know what it's all about yet."

Ruth, as a young girl who certainly did not know what it was all about yet, ventured no comment upon this remark but she was intrigued by the description and wanted badly to view this young man for herself.

The opportunity arose a few weeks later when she and Jessica came walking out of The Bolts onto Main Street and were hailed by a smartly dressed young man. Jessica greeted him somewhat coolly but introduced him to her young cousin, Ruth Buckram. He turned to face the little girl and, bowing slightly, said gravely that he was delighted to make her acquaintance before turning back to Jessica. Ruth could never remember what she said in reply. Normally not in any way a shy girl, she was overcome by this apparition of Godliness. The tall, slender figure, the flaxen hair and eyes of horizon blue all added up to her fanciful idea of a young Viking warrior and yet, to belie that impression, there was the softly spoken greeting, the deference to her (a little girl!) the beautiful clothes and the air of easy elegance. Ruth quite failed to see why her cousin thought so little of her would be suitor and resolved to enquire further into this failing of 'slowness' of which Jessica complained.

But that individual, so described, was now hurrying up Main Street towards his home, having been summarily dismissed by Jessica with an abrupt "We'll say 'Good Morning' then Jonathon." He strode rapidly up Main Street despite the gradient, ruefully considering the lack of success in his advances towards the fisherman's pretty daughter. Oh well there was nothing to be gained from brooding over the matter and he was all the more determined now to settle down to his studies in order to further his overriding ambition. He wanted to be a master mariner and in that desire he was, perhaps surprisingly, aided and abetted by his Aunt Greta. Despite the

tragic loss of her brother and sister-in-law, Greta Stormson
was as fastly joined to the sea as the whole of her family had
been for many generations. She could well understand the
feelings which drove her nephew towards his goal and the
hold which the prospect of seafaring had upon him. As a boy
he had been on short voyages with his father, from which he
had returned bright eyed and ecstatic with pleasure but
fortunately had not been allowed to accompany his parents
on that last fatal journey. As guardian of the boy and the not
inconsiderable fortune which he had inherited, she was more
than ready to fund and assist his endeavours. He was showing
good progress on the theoretical side of things maritime and
soon he was to ship before the mast on the coastal route from
the Tyne to the southern ports. She had no doubt that he
would acquit himself as well practically as he was doing
scholastically. She heard his step on the porch and soon he
was greeting her with a cheery 'Hello Auntie' with no sign of
the disappointment he had just sustained. It was clear that his
life had not been irreparably blighted.

* * * * *

It was a fine October morning and all should have been right
in a world where the bright, low sunlight reflected from the
sea in dazzling fashion and the trees were showing off their
new suit of colours to best advantage. But the brightness,
the gentle lowing of the cattle and the bleating of sheep were
as much as Daniel could take. Any louder noise, including
conversation, was nothing short of an ordeal for the lad after
the previous night's celebration. It had been the occasion of
the wedding of Harry Peacock and Martha Coleman and,
after the solemnity of the service in the little local church
that afternoon, there had been a general letting down of hair
at the wedding breakfast which followed in the village hall
and which lasted long into the evening. Just about everyone
from Highfield and the village were there including both

Mr Farlam and Jane. There had been speeches of course; Mr Farlam himself had been asked to speak on behalf of the bride's family, which he did to great effect. Those who listened carefully were impressed by the way in which he combined humour with respectful congratulation, levity with a serious wish for the happiness of the couple and above all he kept it short enough for his listeners to wish he had spoken longer. When he proposed the health of the happy couple, it was drunk with great enthusiasm and acclaim. Daniel listened intently when Harry replied. Truth to tell he had been nervous on behalf of his friend and erstwhile head horseman and wondered how he would weather the ordeal of speaking to so many people. He need not have worried. Harry spoke simply and naturally. He thanked all for attending, for their presents and above all for their good wishes. He thanked Mr Farlam for his nice speech, the Coleman family for bestowing their daughter upon him and all his friends for their support. He thanked everyone who expected or hoped for thanks and quite a few who had never dreamed of being thanked and the sincerity of his words was obvious to all. High good humour was ensured when he responded to demands and raised his new wife to her feet in order to give her a smacking kiss which drew forth loud applause.

After that the hospitality went on and on, although Mr Farlam and several of the older people left them to it. Jane Farlam stayed on and showed every sign of enjoyment as she participated in the dancing and general merriment, although she refused all offers of alcoholic refreshment. Daniel, no drinker himself, was at pains to keep his intake of alcohol to a reasonable amount despite the encouragement of his fellow horsemen. He somehow contrived to make it appear that he was drinking level with them but managed skilfully to dodge at least one round in three. And it was all good fun – at least at first.

Jane Farlam was having a wonderful time. This was company she enjoyed being with. Good vigorous humour and good vigorous dancing to the old jigs and reels, which were the staple of village entertainment. Daniel was forced to admit to himself that she seemed to be completely at home despite her background of belonging to the landed classes. He was not to know of the boredom which she had suffered in the company of so many of the effete young men whom she met at the soirees and balls, which she attended in the company of her father. Nice enough looking, polite and attentive though they may be, none of them appeared to share her love of the land and things natural. None shared her passion for visiting the wilder parts of the locale, for riding at will across the wide expanses of moorland, for spending quiet hours watching the birds, badgers and foxes. The latter were indeed of interest to some of these young men but only as objects to be chased and harried to their deaths in the company of other hunters splendid in their crimsons and surrounded by the packs of lethal hounds. Jane had taken part in several meets, acquitting herself well as far as the riding was concerned but being so sickened by the eventual climax of the operation that she always deliberately failed to be 'in at the kill'. Although she could see the necessity for the control of the fox she saw no reason why she should be expected to enjoy watching one being torn to pieces. But being the daughter of Richard Farlam she was of course a member of 'the club', moving in a social circle very different to the one she was enjoying so much this evening. The contrast was particularly pleasing to her. The absence of airs and graces, the direct talking and lack of subterfuge or hidden politics and, above all, the happy and energetic dancing instead of the measured and stately dances of the hunt balls, suited her temperament exactly and her occasional shrieks of feigned terror, as she was whirled violently around, did no more than produce sympathetic smiles rather than the raised eyebrows and disapproving glances, which would have been the inevitable reaction of the social elite. Daniel's eyes were not the only ones to follow her around the floor and she was enthusiastically propositioned for each dance by a host of young men, all of whom she seemed to accommodate without tiring. As she floated past in her cornflower blue dress with hair ribbon to match, he watched in awe and with regret that he didn't have the courage to join the queue himself. And then suddenly she was standing in front of him, her face a tableau of audacious smile and laughing eyes.

"At last Mr Robinson" she cried. "I have tracked you down and cornered you. Are you going to continue to hide from me or will you submit to my pleas for the next dance?"

As he stammered out some feeble protest, she removed from his hand the glass, which he had been holding in front of him like some protective amulet, and placing it on a nearby table whisked him out onto the floor. The fiddlers had already struck up again and he was instantly propelled into a frantic reel. Confused and flustered at first, he soon found his feet, for he was of course as familiar with the dance as she seemed to be herself, and before long he was careering around in enjoyable and mildly dangerous fashion. It was entirely natural that they should have the next dance together, and the next, but a diplomatic Jane pointed him in the direction of an eager young female after that and she was off again with another swain, twirling around so uncontrollably that her ribbon came quite out of her hair and the long tresses fell down and swirled around her waist. The very sight of that lovely hair had just fortified Daniel in his determination to win her for another dance, when there was an interruption as a groom appeared at the door. Richard Farlam had decided that enough respect had been accorded to the local revels and he had sent the trap to bring his daughter home. Jane left without demur but not before exchanging noisy farewells and expressions of thanks for her enjoyable evening. As she bent to retrieve her fallen ribbon and was ushered out by the groom, there wasn't a single lad there who, given the amount of alcohol he had taken aboard, wouldn't have offered to lay down his life for her or a single mother who wouldn't have taken her into her arms and given her a hug.

As Daniel watched her retreating back and stared sightlessly into the colossal void caused by her departure, he overheard words of commendation for the young Miss Farlam's willingness to spend so much time in their company before returning to the comforts of the Hall.

"Aye an' that's it" he thought sadly. She had stepped back over the dividing line which had for a while disappeared but was now re-established and separating him irrevocably from her. He looked round for his glass and procured a refill. Then sitting alone he abandoned his good intentions and indulged himself in the alcohol and the bitter thoughts. He had been tremendously affected by her close proximity and the reaction of his body had been, if totally natural, somewhat alarming and embarrassing. He wondered if she had noticed. If so she had made no sign or acknowledgement and now she was leaving. She had clearly fulfilled her function as a sop to the feelings of the villagers and workmen and now it was time to return to her world, with never another thought for the folk she had left behind. Just a duty, a social obligation performed with as much grace as could be mustered in order to keep the peasants happy. As he drank deeper and mused further upon his frustration and her duplicity, he perhaps knew in his heart that he did her wrong but the black mood was not to be denied and he damned her with all the rest of the lordly and unfeeling owners of the land upon which he had to labour so long and so hard in order to make his living. Like Daniel, others and for different reasons, were making no attempt to limit their intake of drink with the inevitable results. One such, Dick Chapman had more to celebrate than the nuptials of Harry and Martha. From that day on Harry would be living out and he, Dick Chapman, had been confirmed as the new waggoner; top dog, overseer of the work and lives of all the horse lads. It was a heady situation to contemplate and he did so with more and more ale. Before long he was leaning on some of the lads with promises of changes and greater discipline and with threats of what would happen, if they failed to meet his standards. Daniel came in for his share of criticism and threats as to what would occur if he failed in his new position as thirdy, but, to the surprise of many, he quite failed to be provoked. It appeared to the onlookers that he was ignoring the gibes of his tormentor and was contemplating some other enemy, invisible to the rest, and so of course he was. To Dick Chapman however, who was now sinking fast into his self imposed swamp of inebriation, it was clear that he had humbled and thoroughly cowed his perceived rival, the upstart young Daniel Robinson. He was of course mistaken.

* * * * *

But now it was the next day, a beautiful day, if one could ignore the fiendish squeal of the badly greased axle or the jarring and clanking of the appliances, as they were hauled across the yard and out through the gate. Dick's snarled rebukes and complaints were suspended only as they passed the waiting group of Mr Farlam and George Buckram but they were resumed as soon as he thought them to be out of earshot. Daniel was regretting many things this morning; the lack of temperance which had produced his splitting headache, the loss of their former waggoner, who had been replaced by a man seemingly determined to make their lives a misery and, oddly, his recriminatory thoughts about the supposed devious behaviour of his late dancing partner. Perhaps this latter change of heart had something to do with the smile and cheery wave she had just given the teams as she cantered off down the lane towards Whitby.

As the months went by all the horse lads were to regret the passing of the old order. Dick Chapman had the devil's own ingenuity in devising unpleasant tasks for those who were not in favour at the moment and indeed for harassing them on a continuous basis throughout the working day. Everyone knew that there had to be a waggoner, a head man from whom direction was received, and everyone was accustomed to the discipline which was necessary to maintain an efficient team. Daniel sometimes likened it to the severe discipline which his brother Tom had told him about in the navy but in truth it was nothing like as hard as that. Nobody was flogged or hung at the yardarm and furthermore the discipline was largely self regulated rather than imposed upon them. The hierarchy had to be maintained to preserve stability and one could not expect to be given the obedience of underlings if one was not prepared to give it to a superior. Even so there had to be a certain amount of respect for that superior and there usually was, because of greater experience and a proven ability to lead competently. Daniel was sure he could carry out the job of waggoner in a far better manner than Chapman, for whom he had no love and little respect. Just one attribute was to be admired. There was no gainsaying that Chapman's team of horses always looked in superb condition and he received regular praise from George Buckram for this. Daniel was impressed too but often wondered how it was achieved. As Waggoner of course, he had control of the feeding of all the horses and would doubtless make sure that his team received their proper share. But it went further than that in as much as they looked so beautifully groomed, their coats glistening in the morning light. Daniel could only suppose that Dick's young lad was working overtime to keep them looking so good. Certainly Dick spent no more time than himself or indeed any of the lads on the welfare of their horses. Meanwhile Daniel's growing feeling of restlessness and dissatisfaction bade fair to destroy the enjoyment of that lovely autumn morning. It was well recognised that employment as a horse lad was regarded as a temporary occupation for young men to mature and acquire experience in farming. Those with ambition might well seek to move on after a year or two with a view to seeking a position as waggoner or maybe foreman of another, but perhaps smaller, farm. Daniel was well aware of these possibilities and had considered them. The problem was that he was loath to leave an occupation for which he was so well suited. If he left Highfield where might he expect to go? There were precious few establishments in this part of the North Riding which could support a labour force solely dedicated to the caring for horses and he could not bear the idea of no longer working with them. The only employer remotely near to Mr Farlam in this respect was his Lordship and he'd be damned if he would ever work for that heartless devil.

It was in February that there came an answer to his problem, a climax to his barely controlled enmity with Chapman and a change in his employment. There had been a succession of heavy frosts and Daniel had paid late visits to the stables on several evenings to make sure that his horses were comfortable and well. He had noted on each occasion that Dick Chapman had also been there, making much of the fact that he was seeing to the welfare of his team and even carrying out a bit of grooming. Daniel had been struck by the smell of burning and Chapman explained that he had been carrying out a little gentle singeing to encourage growth of new hair. This was not unknown as an occasional practice but Daniel had noted that every time he went in to the stables this same smell of burnt hair pervaded the atmosphere. Remembering something his father had once told him, he began to form suspicions as to what might be actually going on and he resolved to keep his eyes open for further clues. The clue when it came was shocking in its intensity. Entering the stable one night, Daniel became aware of a disturbance in the stall accommodating one of Chapman's horses. Hurrying along to see what was the matter, he was concerned to see that Samson, the big bay gelding, was shivering violently and his muscles were going into involuntary contraction. The animal's eyes were rolling, showing only the whites and he was clearly in distress with sweat pouring off him. Dangerous as it was, Daniel entered the stall and tried to calm and comfort the big horse. As he held its head and spoke soothingly into its ears, his eyes searched around the stall and lighted upon a little bottle half buried in the hay at one end of the manger. Gently, and with one hand still holding the horse, he fished out the bottle. He needed both hands to remove the stopper so, letting go of the animal, he did so and his suspicions were immediately confirmed. The smell of aniseed was unmistakable and not masked by any overpowering smell of burnt hair. As he contemplated this a rough voice thundered

"What the devil are ye doin' wi' my 'orse, Robinson?"

It was of course Chapman and despite the poor light from the guarded lantern Daniel could see that his face was suffused with rage. He faced the man squarely nonetheless.

"I'm doin' me best to calm this poor animal as you've been givin' drugs to Dick " he rejoined, confronting the waggoner with the bottle.

"You'll mind yer own bloody business lad; and give me that 'ere."

Anticipating the grab for the bottle, Daniel snatched his hand smartly away. What he did not anticipate was the swinging fist, which was delivered immediately after the words, but his evasive action had saved him from the full effect of the blow. Dropping the bottle he sprang forward to deliver his own riposte, hitting Dick squarely on the chin, but, before he could follow up his advantage, fate took a hand. Samson, stimulated by all this activity, recovered sufficiently to register the fact that he was in some sort of danger and responded in the only way he knew how. He lashed out with a hoof. It was as well that his effort was blind and poorly co-ordinated. The blow to Daniel was a glancing one and bereft of the usual power, which was capable of killing at that range. Even so it was serious enough and Daniel both felt and heard the cracking of the rib which took the main force. He collapsed on the floor but was almost immediately hauled to his feet by the incensed Chapman.

"By God me lad but ye've bin askin' for this for a time and now yer goin' to get it."

Chapman knocked Daniel to the floor with a flailing fist, picked him up again and delivered another blow to a head which was now swimming in a fog of pain and giddiness. Daniel fell again, was dragged to his feet again and would doubtless have received another punishing blow had not the proceedings been interrupted by a stern voice which enjoined them to stop their activities at once. It was George Buckram and he demanded to know just what was going on. Daniel was in no shape to offer any explanation but Dick Chapman seized his opportunity and rounded indignantly upon his foreman.

"I wus just puttin' this young lad in 'is place, George." he replied. "Little bugger was interferin' wi' my 'orse and criticising the way I look after 'im" he offered as further explanation.

But George Buckram had been around a long, long time. If the agitated, sweating animal was not sufficient evidence, the faint smell of aniseed which he had picked up was and he cast around until he spotted the bottle on the floor. He stooped down to pick it up to examine it.

"Tha's bin usin' butter of antimony Dick" he said mildly.

"Aye, well it doesn't do 'em no harm and they looks the better for it" the waggoner said defiantly.

"Nay lad, anyone can see yon animal is in trouble" said George quietly "An' that's why its agin' the law. But law or not its what 'appens 'ere at this farm as matters most. So we'll be goin' up t't Hall for a word wi' Mr Farlam."

Supporting the clearly distressed Daniel with one arm, he pushed Dick Chapman out of the stable and steered the small party up to the Farlam residence. On this cold, clear winter night the bell sounded unnaturally loud and it was quite quickly answered by Richard Farlam himself who, although astonished by this late visitation, admitted them and saw them through into the kitchen where the fire was still glowing.

"Well George" he enquired as he surveyed the group before him. The latter cleared his throat to reply when there was an interruption as the door opened to admit Jane who had heard the disturbance. As all the maids had been given leave to go to bed sometime earlier, she moved immediately to the fire and set about reviving its flames. Her presence was briefly acknowledged by all and then "Yes George what is it?" prompted the foreman again. The tale was soon told and as it unfolded Chapman could tell by the developing expression on the face of his employer that the omens for him were not good. Nothing was calculated to upset the owner of Highfield farm more than the abuse of his precious horses and anyone who could be deemed guilty of such a crime was beyond the pale. It was not such a surprise then that Dick Chapman received his marching orders on the spot. He was advised to leave the area forthwith and seek employment elsewhere because his misdemeanour would be made known to all of the likely employers in the district. Surprisingly there was little real rancour in this dismissal. Chapman had made a serious mistake in the eyes of his employer but it had been one of judgement. Of course his action had been illegal but there was a general acceptance that, however misguided, the idea had been to produce a well turned out horse. Personal profit had never entered the equation and the crime was one of misapplied zeal, unacceptable to the owner and justified as such by the unfortunate reaction of the individual animal, but understandable to many in its motivation. George was instructed to make an accurate calculation of the pay due to him and, when this had been done, Mr Farlam left the room briefly to return with the cash in hand. Handing it over he instructed his former waggoner to return to the farm house and make preparations to leave immediately after breakfast. Accepting the money with a nod and a muttered

"Thank 'ee Mr Farlam", Dick left, never to be seen by them again. Rather than face the awkwardness of questions at breakfast, the general conjecture about what he should do and the lack of sympathy, which he knew would be his due, he packed up his few belongings and walked out into the cold night with not another word.

Meanwhile attention now had focused upon Daniel, who had been leaning silently against the old kitchen dresser with one hand clutching his chest. The abrasions on his face were obvious enough but it was Jane who, noticing his pallor and awkward stance, divined that there was something more to his injuries and pushing past the two men she guided a reluctant Daniel to a chair by the fire. His gasp of pain as he sat was apparent to everyone and George started forward. "Aye, o' course tha wus kicked by yon 'orse wasn't tha lad."

"T'weren't Samson's fault" was the ready reply. "Poor 'orse didn't know what it was doin'."

"Mebbe so lad, but ah'll warrant he'll 'ave left 'is mark."

Reaching Daniel's side George pulled open the shirt to reveal the huge bruise, which was already beginning to discolour the chest. Gently but firmly his fingers explored the site until a gasp of pain helped to confirm his findings and the answer to the unspoken question.

"Aye, there's one rib gone at least, but it could 'ave bin worse." Turning to Mr Farlam he continued. "The lad needs attention sir, could be dangerous to leave a broken rib floatin' about as might puncture 'is lung."

"Yes, of course. We must send for Doctor McClaren straight away." agreed Farlam but his words were countermanded by Jane, who called over her shoulder as she left the room, "No need for that father. His chest just needs binding and we have plenty of old sheets and bandages to do that." The silence after she left was eventually broken by a pensive Mr Farlam who spoke his thoughts aloud.

"Well this has been a bad night to be sure. I have just lost my waggoner and now it seems I shall be looking for a new thirdy as well."

The words struck Daniel like a musket shot, arousing him from the drowsy state into which he had fallen before the fire. Like a cold shower the realisation of his physical condition and all that it implied sank into him and filled him with alarm. At that very moment he realised the truth of his feelings about his situation at Highfield. He desperately wanted to stay. All his mental posturing about the loss of his father's farm was put into perspective and revealed for what it was, a childish dream, a rosy coloured image of a way of life, which had been hard and financially unrewarding. Here at Highfield he had been happy. He had been doing a man's job at work which he enjoyed, amongst animals he loved; he had earned the respect of employer and colleagues and he had been well fed and housed. The prospect of having to leave all this appalled him. Daniel suddenly had a new insight into his own personality. He knew himself to be independent, obstinate, hard and proud. His carefully cultivated self reliance was an integral part of that pride but he found now that he was prepared to abandon that in this moment of truth. He was prepared to beg. He opened his mouth to do so and the impassioned words spilled out.

"Nay, please Mr Farlam. If I'm well strapped up I'll be able to work the horses at least. Mebbe not so much liftin' but that won't be for long. Please don't turn me off now."

The struggle of emotions upon his face had been so evident that Mr Farlam, who had by now formed a pretty good assessment of the lad's character for himself, laughed out loud, whilst acknowledging quietly to himself the sacrifice of pride which had just been made. The laughter silenced Daniel, had begun to anger him indeed, but the next words astonished him.

"No Daniel you are not to leave but you do need to recover. No working until the doctor pronounces you fit enough and then light duties for a while. Mind you I shall want no backsliding or shirking once you're back on the job."

The smile on his face took the sting out of that admonition and Jane, who had just returned with armfuls of bandaging material, was conscious of a very different atmosphere in the room. It was convivial, almost jovial and as she knelt to help Daniel out of his shirt and apply her nursing skills she received her own instructions from her father.

"Now Jane, see you make a good job of this. You are tending to my new waggoner and I want him back at work as soon as possible."

Daniel sat spellbound and incredulous. The background conversation between Mr Farlam and George drifted past him, with details of how the foreman was to assume the duties of waggoner temporarily, whilst Farlam himself would enter more fully into the working management of the farm to help him out. A search would be implemented for a new horse lad to make up the numbers and there would be promotion for the fourther to thirdy, he having demonstrated his abilities and steadiness in recent months. Daniel registered all this almost subliminally. At the top of his mind there was so much to think and rejoice about. He was to be waggoner at last, or more truthfully, rather sooner than he had been able to hope for. This had been his first ambition, the most important in fact as he had stood in line at the hirings in Whitby that day. Now he had achieved it and there was the possibility of imagining further advances, given hard work and a lot of luck. A foreman needed wisdom and lots of experience but that was something which time could bring about. Meanwhile the touch of a tendril of golden hair brushing against his face and the scent of this lovely young woman, whose arms were passing around his body with the bandages, combined with the drowsiness instilled by the warmth of the fire to reduced him to a state of sleepy euphoria, all discomfort banished by the wonder of his new circumstances.

There was just the one thing to spoil the pleasure. He had been induced to beg, to implore his employer for his continued position at Highfield and unnecessarily so it seemed. It was a weakness that he would not allow himself to indulge in again.

CHAPTER 3

THE WAGGONER

The spring of 1868 had begun cold and wet on the North Yorkshire Moors and no more so than on the coastal strip where harsh winds from the north east swept over the cliffs lowering the temperature in terms of the way it actually felt, still allowing growth but depressing the spirits of the inhabitants. Despite this there was an aura of reasonable contentment amongst most of the population on the Highfield estate. True the weather had been bad, the land had been difficult to manage and the new born lambs had suffered severely in the harsh conditions. Mortality had been high amongst the flocks but the weather had at least ensured a good growth of grass and if only the hay crop could be gathered in safely the situation for the following winter would be assured. The trouble was that the rain showed little sign of abating and whilst things were not yet desperate there was cause to worry a little.

Daniel sat upon Bess and contemplated the saturated ground. In two weeks it would be June, the traditional time to harvest the clover crop on the low pasture. Unless things improved dramatically there would be no clover crop. But there was time yet. Daniel like all who lived in this area knew of the vagaries of the weather and how it could change so quickly. What exercised his mind was not so much the immediate future but what he should plan to do for the following year. He was the waggoner; had been so for over two years now. Once the limit of his ambition, he was happy in this job but in five months he would be forced to make a decision. He was confident that he could be re-appointed in his present position. He felt had given every cause for satisfaction but should he stay? Many of his contemporaries had moved on from the occupation of horse boy and perhaps it was time for him to do likewise. With his experience and with a favourable reference from Mr Farlam he might expect to get a position as foreman on a smaller farm and he was sure George Buckram would also speak for him and offer advice too when the time came for him to move on. But there was time to think more on the problem during the rest of the summer and meanwhile he was content with his lot. It seemed that George was delegating to him some of the work normally undertaken by the foreman – not a great deal but enough to make Daniel feel that he had been assessed as a responsible person and this pleased him.

As for George Buckram, he too was pleased to be able to pass on some of the load to his young and vigorous waggoner. Discipline among the horse lads was no problem; Daniel kept them very much in check and had established a reputation for being tough but fair. He drove them hard but no harder than he worked himself. George was well pleased with the state of affairs and especially his now greater involvement with the horse breeding programme. Nowadays he spent some time at the Hall discussing policy with his employer rather than merely overseeing the management of the men and their activities. For his part Richard Farlam was also enjoying this stronger relationship with his old and trusted employee. He valued his advice when it was offered and placed a good deal of faith in his judgement. Having hitherto taken the responsibility for his plans entirely on his own he found it quite pleasant to have another person share his ideas and submit opinions even if he didn't take action on them.

Jane too was happy in a way, still enjoying the freedom of roaming the moors and little valleys on her own, and yet somehow conscious of a vague feeling of restlessness. She felt that there was something missing in her life although she found it impossible to identify just what this was. Unable to do so therefore, she simply put it right to the back of her mind and enjoyed her life for what it was.

In the old farmhouse there was an equal sense of contentment. The lads were kept busy and therefore out of mischief. Alice Buckram had no trouble with any of them and she went on in her own quiet and purposeful way as she had always done. The only person to feel any heightened feelings in this generally placid community was young Ruth Buckram. For her something quite momentous was to happen in a few weeks time. She was to be bridesmaid to her cousin Jessica and all of her spare time was now spent in the cottage at Bay Town where plans were laid and much cutting out and sewing was being done. They had agonised together on the colour scheme and choice of material for they had indeed had a choice. Uncle Jethro had announced that no expense would be spared in turning his daughter out in real style at her wedding. With only one bridesmaid and therefore only two dresses to fund he had been able to provide enough cash to make the girls giddy with the choices that opened up to them. Ruth marvelled at the generosity of her uncle. She knew well enough the dangers and hardships which attended the winning of a living from the sea. She had stood alongside Aunt Martha as wrapped in her shawl and bonnet, her face battered by the wind and rain, they watched and prayed for the cobbles to reach the safety of the landing through the mountainous seas. Sometimes it was impossible and the boats had to stand off until the sea had moderated sufficiently to allow them to attempt a landing and for those on shore these periods of waiting seemed to last a lifetime. The skippers always made sure of having sufficient sea room and so it needed a good glass to watch them, even if the conditions of visibility allowed, but Ruth had once been permitted a look through the coast guard's telescope and had been terrified at the sight of the cobbles as they battled against the gigantic swells which marched across the bay. She was told the seas were running at about thirty feet and could well believe it. Time and time again a boat would disappear into a trough and stay hidden until she thought it lost for good only for it to reappear with water sloughing over the stern boards, the oilskin clad occupants barely visible as they clung on grimly. And Ruth had shared those times when continuous storms had made fishing impossible, with a consequent lack of income. Even worse, those storms were often responsible for loss of gear and she had helped with the cutting of hazels when a whole new fleet of pots had had to be made as quickly as possible so as to restore the family's earning ability. Combining this with the vagaries of the market it all added up to an incredibly precarious living which was wrought from these coastal waters. And yet Uncle Jethro and Simeon seemed to enjoy the life with no desire to change their occupation and thus it was for most if not all of the fishing families in Robin Hood's Bay. The impending wedding was set to establish a link between the Jensons and another family long connected with the sea and inshore fishing, for Jessica was to wed Ned Brewster a lad well known and well liked in the little community. Ruth had met him several times and found him to be very lively and cheerful, not by any means the sort to earn her cousin's categorisation of 'slow'. In fact the wedding had had to be brought forward a month or so for reasons, which everyone knew of but nobody spoke about nor acknowledged in any way; except that Ruth had noticed her aunt was stockpiling some small squares of cloth for an undesignated purpose.

As she worked at the little kitchen table Ruth was enjoying the atmosphere of happiness and expectation. The men folk were even chirpier than usual and the torrent of jokes and leg pulling never stopped. Ruth too came in for her share of it and she was reminded more than once that this would be her big chance to show herself off and catch the eye of a likely lad. Whilst she protested her lack of intention to do anything of the sort, Ruth had in fact thought often of that very eventuality and she nursed to herself the idea that some handsome youth might pay her attention and admire her lovely dress. It was certainly a part of her excited anticipation of the event.

And that event was undeniably a complete success. Miraculously the weather improved and on the day it was sunny and dry if a trifle cool. At the Jensen household there had been a tense period earlier in the year when an apparent impasse had been reached between the mother and father of the bride. Martha, a staunch supporter of the established church, had made it abundantly clear that, whilst she enjoyed very good relations with her Methodist neighbours, she would be insisting on her daughter marrying within the bosom of mother church, the family church of St Stephens on Thorpe Road in the village of Fylingdales at the top of the bank. This was where they had married, where their children had all been christened and there was a perfectly adequate church hall in which the wedding breakfast could be served. Jethro on the other hand, which he incidentally wagged insistently whilst making his point, was equally clear that, as he was paying the bills, he was going to see to it that all his friends would be able to attend the celebrations and the King's Arms on the Dock was right opposite the chapel. Not being possessed of the same religious scruples as his wife, and even having the temerity to suggest that maybe a change was as good as a rest, the convenience of a situation where the bride and groom accompanied by the congregation, including of course his particular cronies, could march directly from one edifice to another appealed to his sense of order and propriety such that he stuck out for his argument way beyond most disagreements with his wife. The solution when it came was of course a compromise which provided wonderful entertainment for the local community and the source of happy reminiscence for many years to come.

As Ruth marched slowly up the aisle behind her cousin and uncle her little cup was certainly close to overflowing. She was so happy. She was happy for Jessica who was marrying the man she loved and was so obviously enjoying every moment of the occasion; she was happy for her Aunt and Uncle who were clearly very proud of their lovely daughter and revelling in the opportunity to show her off to friends and family; she was happy too herself, grateful to her uncle for providing the material for this beautiful dress the like of which she had never worn before, and in which she imagined she looked quite presentable. It was entirely typical of the girl that her own feelings came last on the list. Hers was a character which thrived upon the happiness and well being of those around her. No task or little kindness was either too trivial or too large for her to undertake in the furtherance of her friends and family's enjoyment. The posy she carried and the bouquet which Jessica sported had been made by Ruth that very morning with flowers picked from the hedgerows around Highfield, as well as blooms from the little cottage garden on The Bolts. An ingenuous blend of cultivation and nature with Red Campions standing bravely alongside Roses and Harebells peeping delicately over the Phlox and yet totally in keeping with the ambience of the rustic old church which had doubtless witnessed many a similar floral tribute over the centuries. The wedding gift which she had diffidently handed to Jessica had been a beautifully worked piece of linen, transformed by her painstaking efforts over many months into a magnificent tablecloth. If she had been surprised and embarrassed by the warmth and genuine gratitude expressed by her cousin, she would have been dumbfounded by the price it was to realise in an auction house a hundred and fifty years later.

She was passing now the pew which housed her parents and she was warmed through and through by the loving smiles they bestowed upon her. It was perhaps a good thing that she was oblivious to the approving comment, which she excited from others in the congregation, several of whom nodded sagely and avowed that she would be the next one to fulfil the principal role in a ceremony such as this for, paragon of the virtues as she may seem from this description, she had her faults one of which was a dreadful shyness. It was based upon a strange lack of self confidence. Perhaps this was born of her comparative isolation at Highfield. There she was confident. She was confident of the love of her parents, confident of the contribution which she could make to the running of the household and the help she could afford her mother in particular. It was only in the wider world outside that her confidence failed her. Her visits to Bay Town and more exceptionally to Whitby only served to make her aware of a surrounding culture which seemed alien in its speed and urgency. Let no one think that hers was an inferior intellect. Rather was it that the plethora of new ideas, modern practices, never had the time or opportunity to impinge upon her lifestyle. Not entirely from her own predilection she was something of a social dinosaur and, being conscious of this, she took a back seat on most public occasions.

Today was different however. Today she could not avoid being thrust forward into the limelight. The actual service in which events followed a well known and well defined procedure was no problem. Ruth enjoyed the predictability of the ceremony; the exchange of vows thrilled her and momentarily she thought of herself and hoped that she too would one day be a part of this wonderful bonding of two people. But the service over, she had to process with the principals back up the nave and into the gaze of the assembled throng outside in the churchyard. Whilst the newly weds were the main centre of attention, her own efforts to disappear into the background were doomed to failure and she was constantly being forced forward to be showered with rose petals. The joy of the occasion and the evident goodwill of the many well-wishers did much to dispel her feeling of awkwardness but, when she suddenly became conscious of appraisal from a well remembered pair of clear blue eyes, her legs became wobbly and she leant upon the side of the porch. It was of course he of the Viking lineage, he of the kind smile and courteous demeanour, he of the sartorial elegance which had so impressed her and who was even now removing his tall hat and bowing towards her. How she hoped that nobody was noticing this preferment. But it was not to stop there! Pushing forward through the throng, Jonathon first congratulated the bride and groom and then confronted her directly, complimenting her in fulsome fashion upon her appearance and apparent good health. There was no one else from whom she would rather have heard those words so why was it that she made such a poor showing in her reply? Her native good manners and parental teaching enabled her to stumble through the conventional responses but it was noticeable that he did not prolong the encounter and she bitterly regretted her inability to capitalise on this meeting. An opportunity had been irretrievably squandered. She had quite failed to observe the smile of understanding and sympathy on his face as he turned away.

The happy couple were now directed to pass under a florally decorated arch which led them onto the church lane where uncle Jethro took over the management of proceedings according to the bargain struck earlier in the year. Here they were handed into a carriage, bedecked with flowers and lined with silks. Small matter that this carriage bore a striking resemblance to Jed Latham's brewer's dray and that their seat lurched rather alarmingly as they sat down. Old Billy, adorned with highly polished brasses and looking a sight cleaner than he had for many a month, was led off by an equally unrecognisable Jed clad in bright red shirt, his best cord breeches and shining leather boots and they commenced their journey through the village and down the hill to the foot of King Street. Progress was necessarily slow as Billy negotiated the steep gradient with his precious cargo but this only allowed the accompanying throng to keep pace with repeated shouts of encouragement. As they slowed even further to tackle some of the sharp bends opportunity was afforded the occupants of first floor windows to shower more flowers and indeed other less conventional objects upon them. The jollity of the occasion was infectious and the sound of their progress preceded them. The folk crowding the narrow streets of Baytown, residents and holidaymakers alike, responded to this regardless of whether they knew the main protagonists or not. In view of the mounting swell of sound and activity it is not surprising that old Billy, more accustomed to a quieter and more prosaic way of life, reacted in uncharacteristic fashion and provided the highlight of the marital progress. It must really have been the stimulus of the human enthusiasm which precipitated the old horse's reaction but whatever the cause, Billy attempted an exaggerated sashay as he rounded the corner past Mr Thomson's emporium with disastrous results. His ill considered gyration caused the rear of the wagon to slide away and the vehicle collided catastrophically with the shop frontage. There was no personal injury to passengers or spectators but, as might be expected, the cascade of glass with its attendant noise evoked mirth and cheers from all except the unfortunate proprietor, who emerged from his devastated premises just in time to shake his fist at the disappearing form of Jethro Jenson. This latter, with the Kings Head in sight, was not to be delayed in his progress and he contented himself, and it must be admitted the injured shopkeeper, with a departing cry of " I'll see you all right, Mr Thomson, I'll see you right." as the cavalcade rounded the last bend on the way to its ultimate destination.

Looking back at the events of the day, as she lay sleepless in her makeshift bed in the cottage on the Bolts, Ruth savoured again that moment and also the celebrations which followed. There was the plentiful supply of plain good fare and drink, the latter being especially approved of and exploited by the fisher folk in the party, there were the speeches, all humorous in content, and there was for Ruth the magic moment when, the wedding cake being cut, the bride and groom met in an embrace and kiss which ignored the assembly and advertised only the love between them. Afterwards, the tide having receded sufficiently, there were the foot races on the beach, when young men and boys competed for the honours and the winner of the open event duly presented himself for the traditional prize. Nothing loath and even with enthusiasm the bride hoisted her skirts and removed her garter to hand it to the victor, who to seal the bargain delivered her a smacking kiss. It was really only a part of the ritual which prescribed the groom's furious intervention, sending the interloper on his way to the delight of the onlookers. It had all been so pleasant, so happy, so according to the tradition in which she had been brought up and Ruth relived the occasion contentedly as she fought off the sleep which she really needed. The one aspect of the day which grieved her was her failure to deal adequately with the meeting with Jonathon Stormson. How she regretted that and wished for an opportunity to make amends. This wished for opportunity was to occur much sooner than she had hoped for.

It was just a fortnight later and Ruth stepped out of the newly refurbished door of Thomsons emporium clutching the heavy shopping basket only to fall immediately into the path of the young gentleman in question. Excusing herself quickly and breathlessly she was interrupted by his own apologies for his clumsiness and felt the shopping bag snatched from her grip. Nothing would please him but the opportunity to carry her bag up the hill on his way, as he explained, to his aunt's house. The conversation, stilted at first, became more animated as they ascended to a point where the sea was visible over the rooftops of the cottages. Ruth had paused to take breath and admire the view of which she never tired. Sensing her mood Jonathon described his own passion for the sea and how it had fascinated him from his earliest days as a boy. His father had taken him for short journeys on the brig and it was a matter of pure chance that he had not accompanied his parents on their last fatal voyage. An examination at school had prevented his participation. He regarded that now as an indication that he had to progress scholastically and take his master's certificate as soon as possible; in some fashion he felt that this was the only way he could honour his father's memory. Looking into his earnest face, the blue eyes fixed upon the horizon, Ruth felt she understood this fixation and sympathised with it; in fact she envied him his certainty as to what he should do with his life. Her own ambitions were unclear, unformed in fact, and she saw nothing further at her stage in life than a continuance of helping out at Highfield Old Farm. Whilst Jonathon loved the sea as a medium upon which he could sail, bending the elements to his will and travelling the world, her own love for it was land based. She enjoyed watching the play of light upon its surface, the change of moods from placid, velvety and seductive companion through its surly and restless stages to the grand fury of an all out storm. Often, she told Jonathon, she had walked out in the wildest weather to view such a storm from the safety of the cliffs above Homerell Hole, one of her favourite vantage points, gazing in awe at the stupendous power of the waves crashing against the shore far below. The sheer elemental power thrilled her as much as the magnificent visual display of spray and broken water. She admitted to a childish feeling of pleasure in being protected by the rampart of rocks whilst the enemy, the sea, tried vainly to assail her position and always retreated baffled. Jonathon for his part saw the sea as a friend, one to be treated with caution to be sure, but a friend who could be relied upon in terms of regularity of tides, currents and manners. Their discussion had so absorbed them, that it was with a laugh that Ruth observed that they had walked way past Jonathon's house. Laughing in turn, he declared that he must make the best of the situation and carry her basket for her all the way to Highfield. Ruth made no protest for she wanted this meeting prolonged to the very end of time. But of course it was finite and Highfield came into sight all too soon. He refused the offer of refreshment as he was already well overdue for his return and with a cheery wave was about to depart, when he stopped and turned towards her. "Ruth" he said " You must take me to your favourite place on the cliffs and show me that view you so love. I am off to sea in a few days but we shall arrange it when I return." With that he swung away down the path leaving a girl who hugged herself with joy at this redemption from the penalties of her gauche behaviour at the wedding. Happiness, she discovered, was a very relative commodity and she was experiencing its heights at that moment. How fortunate she was that she could appreciate this, as things were to change drastically and very quickly for the poor girl.

It is extraordinary how varied are the effects upon a community when one of its members dies. It would be foolish to claim that all are missed equally and it is noticeable that the extent to which they are missed bears little relation to the social standing, wealth or position of the deceased. Sometimes a death is anticipated, even hoped for, as a blessed means of relief; sometimes it is hoped for because of more mercenary considerations; sometimes, very sadly, it is a matter of almost indifference to the community at large, and of great moment to only a few family mourners. But often there may die a person who, whilst not a prime mover and shaker in events local or national, will by their departure cause shock waves which ripple out to affect the courses of many lives as well as inflicting the sorrow attendant upon their demise. Such a person was Alice Buckram, the 'decent little body who was not fortunate with her health', as she was described by Mary Robinson. Unfortunate or not, Alice was not expected to die. It had never occurred to anyone that she might do so. She was an institution which simply kept going, utterly reliable, undemanding and quietly efficient, a permanent feature of the administrative and working practice of Highfield Estate. When it was learnt that she had been found slumped over the full washing basket, which she had probably been attempting to lift, the usual reaction to the news was of stunned disbelief, followed by a profound sorrow and feeling of terrible loss. It was George who had made the discovery and he had lifted her in his arms, carried her into the house and laid her gently on the parlour couch before summoning Ruth to her aid. Without any warning of what she was to find, the girl was devastated and wept uncontrollably over her mother's body. She was conscious of the soothing hand which stroked her hair and after a while looked up to see her father smiling down upon her. She was startled by his apparent control but even more amazed by his next remark.

"Well Ruth, it seems tha' must do the supper tonight. Mother's not up to it."

"But father" she sobbed "We've lost her; she's gone!"

"Nay lass, if you start the supper I'll just pop out to the stable for a minute or so."

Ruth stared in horror at his retreating form and called him back again.

"Father you can't just go out now, there'll be, well, things to do and people to notify."

"Now Ruth, I am very busy, we all are, and you must be ready to help your mother out whilst she is not herself."

He left abruptly and Ruth was appalled by his reaction. Clearly he was not registering the fact that his wife was dead. After a few seconds to gather her thoughts, she ran quickly up to the Hall to tell them the tragic news. Mr Farlam was shocked and very sympathetic. He enquired how she was feeling herself and received assurance that she was all right and could cope. "But it's father sir" she stammered. "I can't seem to get him to understand that mother has gone, that –"

she stumbled over the words with a sob, "That she's – dead." That was the first time she had used the word and it brought home the horror of the situation more fully. "I don't rightly know what to do about things, I mean arrangements and all that, and father doesn't seem to take any notice of what's happened. He thinks she is just poorly or something and tells me to get on and help her get the supper ready" She started to cry in earnest now and Richard Farlam was beginning to grasp the dreadful situation the young girl was in. With a father whose mind had been disturbed by the tragedy she had nobody to turn to – except of course himself. He bethought him of his own daughter too and summoned her. Duties were assigned and off they all went, Farlam to the stables to interview his foreman, Jane and Ruth to the farmhouse to deal with matters there whilst a groom was despatched to fetch the doctor. Ruth looked askance at this latter command but Mr Farlam explained the necessity for a medical opinion to be laid before the coroner and she was grateful for the way her father's employer had taken over and started to make all the necessary arrangements. Quietly and gently Jane helped to move the body into the bedroom and enquired of Ruth if she wanted help with the laying out.

"I think Aunt Martha will want to come and see to it Miss Jane" said Ruth looking worried.

"Of course, we must tell her immediately" replied Jane. "I'll send one of the grooms down directly if you'll just give me their address. Now Ruth, those hungry lads will be coming in directly, do you think you can manage to get their supper tonight?"

"Oh yes, Miss Jane, I can do that all right".

The reply was pathetically grateful for Ruth wanted nothing better than to concentrate on some simple job and erase from her mind as far as possible the dreadful events she had experienced. Jane, who had guessed that this would be the best medicine, smiled encouragingly and told Ruth to send up to the Hall if she needed any help but, staying to watch for a little while, she saw that Ruth was dealing with matters in a perfectly competent fashion and left her to it. As Jane was walking back to the Hall, she noticed the figure of George hurrying back from the stable block to the old farmhouse. She hesitated for a moment but decided that this was not the time to accost him and offer her sympathy so she continued home and awaited the arrival of her father. When he did return a few minutes later he looked very agitated and wore a baffled expression.

"I don't know what to make of the man!" he said to Jane. "I found him busying himself in the stable at something which could well have awaited a more propitious time and when I spoke to offer my sympathy on the loss of Alice he just smiled and assured me she would be all right. I tried again to find words which would bring the truth home to him but after a while he interrupted me to say that he was sorry he couldn't stay to chat because Alice was not very well and she needed his help in the house. With that he raised his hat and made off without another word! I'm sorry to say it but I believe his mind has been totally unhinged by the shock and the realisation of the truth when it dawns will be a terrible experience for him. We must watch him carefully."

Jane agreed and said also that Ruth would bear watching too. They debated whether or not to send one of the maids down to help but Jane counselled against this. She had been impressed with the purposeful way in which the girl had set about the preparations for the meal and knew that this activity was therapeutic. The fact was however, that she was labouring under the double blow of the loss of her mother's life and her father's rationality so she would certainly need some moral support and company. Jane resolved to make regular calls upon the farmhouse in future.

A few days later there was a small conference in the study at the Hall comprising Richard Farlam, Jane and Andrew McClaren the doctor. They had all attended the sombre little

funeral service in the church, where only a few short weeks
before there had been such a happy occasion, when Alice
had enjoyed the wedding of her niece. Andrew McClaren
had been present specifically at the request of Richard Farlam
in order to speak to and observe George Buckram. He was
telling them now of that conversation and how totally
befuddled George had appeared to be.

"He seemed to think he was participating in a wedding.
When I asked him whose he told me it was Ruth and yet she
had been sitting beside him. On two occasions he addressed
his daughter and called her Alice. There is no doubt about
it; he has become completely deranged by the shock of his
wife's death and his mind is quite refusing to accept the fact.
I am afraid that I cannot tell you how long this will last, indeed
he might never regain his sanity."

The doctor went on to say that George was likely to remain
affable and harmless but disassociated from the real world
and therefore not reliable as far as his work was concerned.

"Then I'm going to need a new foreman" said Farlam
grimly.

"But father you can't just turn out George and Ruth after
all the years of service he and his family have given!" Jane
was indignant, almost wrathful, but she was reassured
immediately.

"No Jane, there's no question of that. It seems that young
Ruth is coping very well with her duties and with George to
help her carry out more physically demanding jobs I see no
reason to disturb them. But a new foreman I must have. I
shall hire one and he can sleep out."

The doctor now took his leave, wishing them well and
regretting silently to himself that a small sherry or something
more potent had not been offered during their discourse.
But he recalled that from his own previous experience, and
indeed that of others he had talked to, that there seemed to

be no alcohol of any kind kept at Highfield. Meanwhile Jane and her father had reconvened their meeting and were discussing the options. It was Jane who came up with the suggestion that Daniel Robinson be offered the job of foreman. Mr Farlam raised several objections; he was very young for the job with no previous experience, he was a good waggoner and it would be difficult to replace him. Jane countered these arguments with her own. Some months ago she had heard George himself say that Daniel was a great help and would one day make a good foreman; he had even warned that, from clues he had picked up, the lad might be seeking such a position elsewhere at the end of this year. The loss of waggoner and foreman together in one year would be a difficult situation with which to deal. Furthermore George had commented favourably upon the new-found reliability of Jed Barker, the current thirdy. Whilst still a lively character, he had matured and his attitude had improved under the influence of his waggoner. Perhaps he could be made up to waggoner? Richard Farlam listened in amazement to these suggestions. He had had no idea that his daughter was so well informed and so interested in the working of the estate. He considered her ideas and found little to object to, providing he could overlook the youthfulness of his prospective new foreman and always providing of course that Daniel would accept the position. Further reflection convinced him that there would be no problem in that respect however. He promised Jane that he would give the matter further thought but that her ideas seemed sound and he might well follow them through.

Thus it was, that Daniel found himself perched uncomfortably and very much ill at ease on a chair in the sitting room of the Hall, the first time in fact that he had penetrated the inner sanctum of the great house. With due warning of this evening meeting, he had completed his toilet very thoroughly and was clad in his best shirt and breeches with immaculately polished leather leggings. His boots shone and he twiddled his cap nervously in his fingers as he listened to what his employer had to say. He was, to say the least, surprised and excited by this offer. It was the answer to his own uncertainties about his future. Not only was he to become a foreman but foreman of Highfield, the largest farm in the area! He was familiar with most of the practices on the farm and would soon pick up more knowledge from George. He paused there in his thoughts with the realisation that George might not be the helpful source that he had been in the past. But he did have his lucid moments and could talk sensibly about the farm work. Daniel's ruminations were interrupted as Mr Farlam explained his intentions for the immediate future. Martinmas was two months away and existing contracts would continue until then. Meanwhile Daniel was to combine as best he could his responsibilities as waggoner and acting foreman. Mr Farlam was making a generous increase in his wage to compensate for this extra work and responsibility. He was also instructed to groom Jed Barker for the job of waggoner in November should he want that. Daniel grinned involuntarily.

"He'd give his back teeth for it sir!" he said and they all laughed appreciatively.

"Well now Daniel I took the liberty of anticipating your acceptance of the job and I have prepared a list of all the duties I shall expect you to carry out as foreman. There is also a written contract for you to peruse and sign if you are satisfied with the terms."

Farlam leant across and handed the document to Daniel with a smile but there was a noticeable hesitation before it was accepted. Daniel recovered quickly and overcoming his embarrassment answered the unspoken question.

"Thank you sir, thank you but I've never had much to do with writing and papers and the like. I'm sure though that if you've written it then it'll be all right."

Jane leapt into the short but awkward silence.

"That's fine Daniel but I think we should perhaps go over it, perhaps tomorrow evening if I could come down to the farmhouse?"

She gave her father a warning glance and he remained silent as she ushered Daniel out.

Richard Farlam was pensive when she returned.

"That's a new disadvantage which we hadn't considered. He cannot read or write can he?"

"No father, it seems he cannot but is that such a grave disadvantage?" she enquired.

"Yes Jane, I'm afraid it is. He will need to be numerate at least and be able to read bills of sale etc. I may have to reconsider."

"Let's find out first just how much he can do in that respect father" Jane protested. "It may be that he needs just a little coaching – I'm sure he is bright enough but he has never had the cause or opportunity to have a formal education. Let me see what I can discover tomorrow evening and I will report back to you."

That plan was agreed and on the following evening after supper Jane attended the farmhouse and met with Daniel in the seclusion of the parlour. She started by explaining that she had thought he might have difficulty with some of the strange legal expressions in the document and she could perhaps go over it with him. Without any delay she set about reading from the paper, which in truth contained nothing difficult at all, but she made a point of stopping to discuss with him the implications of some of the terms of the agreement and also the instructions as to his duties. When they had finished Daniel expressed his gratitude and Jane, with a friendly smile, handed him the papers and then asked

"Daniel, tell me frankly and in confidence, how much of that paper could you actually read for yourself?"

Only a fraction of a second's pause and then came the rueful reply, "Not a lot, Miss Jane. I can read a few words like my own name – I can write it too- and I think I can recognise some of the smaller words and some words as I have seen written down under the pictures in my mother's bible."

"Yes, I see Daniel." Jane spoke in matter of fact fashion with no suspicion of condescension or criticism. "I should think there was very little need for that sort of teaching in your job – too many other things to learn about managing the horses, ploughing and all the other skills you have acquired."

"That's right Miss! It was all hard work on my father's farm; difficult to work it was, and there was no time for proper schooling but, God willing, I was to be tenant after my father in time. I really wanted that but it was not to be."

The bleak expression on his face warned her not to continue the discussion on this topic so she changed the subject directly and went straight to the point.

"Daniel, my father thinks it most important that you be able to read and write at least to the extent of dealing with merchants, ordering and checking supplies, all that sort of work which you will in future be dealing with. Otherwise he feels he will probably have to reconsider his offer."

Recognising the bitter disappointment in his features she continued quickly " But we can easily get over that problem. I can give you a bit of help each evening until you can catch up and we'll soon have you able to cope with anything of that sort in your work."

The smile which transformed his face caused her heart to turn over at that moment. What a handsome young animal he was to be sure!

"Oh Miss Jane, if you could spare the time I would really like to do that. Not just because I really want the job of foreman but because I was always sorry not to have done my schooling properly. I was the elder you see, I was to be gaffer on the farm whilst my younger brother, Tom, had less interest and was allowed to go to school till he was twelve years old! He can read and write properly" he said with some pride, "that's why they took him in the navy."

"I should like to meet your brother Daniel" Jane commented and knew it was the best thing she could have said for the lad went on about his younger sibling in glowing terms.

"He were never a great hard worker, our Tom, bit of a prankster, always getting into scrapes but he is a lot of fun. Not like me you see Miss. I know I seem a bit serious like and dull but our Tom always makes me smile. Even my parents had to smile sometimes when they should by rights have been telling him off good and proper. Anyway, now he's in the navy and we see little enough of him but he says it is a good life."

Daniel was suddenly conscious of the fact that he had been loquacious well beyond his normal practice and covered his confusion by leaping up and offering to make a drink for his guest. Jane refused, but warmly and regretfully, saying that she needed to return to the Hall and discuss their plans with her father. A brief handshake and she left with the words "Tomorrow evening up at the Hall then Daniel, after supper."

After she had left, Daniel contemplated his tingling palm and his mind replayed the evening's conversation. Terribly conscious of the tremendous gulf between them, he was astounded at the ease with which he had spoken to her and how she had listened and understood him and his feelings. Upper class, well above his station maybe, but she was so very approachable and sympathetic. And she was beautiful. He admitted that to himself as though it was something about which he should never think. Daniel found himself looking forward to his lesson on the morrow with something more than a mere desire to further his education.

* * * * *

It was a wild and exhilarating ride through the short bracken with the wind singing in his ears. The horse he bestrode was a beautiful hunter, by far the most elegant and speedy animal he had ever ridden but, fast though it was, he had difficulty keeping up with the girl he accompanied. It had been Jane who had made the suggestion, insisted in fact, that they break off from their lesson and enjoy the sunshine whilst they could on this lovely October day. She had chafed a little over her protege's dedication to his work when the good weather was passing them by and she had made her protest when he arrived at the Hall that Sunday afternoon her father being out socialising with the local gentry. Jane had been amused by the play of conflicting emotions which passed across the open countenance before her. Disappointment that his learning progress was to be checked, excitement at the prospect of riding a well bred horse and perhaps a slight embarrassment at the prospect of indulging in an activity which was considered to be the provenance of the wealthy classes. The prospect of the ride in the company of this vivacious and lovely girl however easily overcame the protests of his conscience and the expedition was immediately arranged. Jane had been surprised and pleased by the enthusiasm with which Daniel had entered into his tuition in reading and writing. He had taken it in as a parched traveller would drink water and had made impressive progress over the few weeks in which he had been engaged in the process. He had been in the habit of attending the Hall on one or two evenings each week and occasionally on a Sunday afternoon. They had worked in the study with great dedication to the task in hand and totally ignoring old Betsy, whose function as chaperone was somewhat impaired by her tendency to drop off into a sound sleep which lasted for the duration of the lesson. Between times, she had heard, he laboured every night by candlelight practising his writing and trying to read simple texts which he proudly repeated for her at their next meeting. Jane was indeed highly gratified by this justification of her confidence in the young man and Richard Farlam, who had on occasion peeped in through the study door, had smiled in appreciation of his efforts, nodding conspiratorially with his daughter before silently closing the door. It became quickly obvious to Jane that his potential for success had already been there, that he had imbibed at least the basics from his perfunctory attendance at school or perhaps from his brother's example. She definitely had the impression that he was not starting completely from scratch but, having said that, his progress was still remarkable. And his appetite for improvement was insatiable, so much so that she found his requests for more and more tuition encroaching steadily upon her own leisure time. But these requests were made with an unstudied and ingenuous diffidence, which quite failed to mask the underlying enthusiasm, and the appeal was irresistible. Furthermore, she discovered to her surprise that she had not the slightest regret for some of the social engagements she had cancelled and was beginning to think that her leisure time could not be more pleasantly spent.

So here they were now enjoying the physical exercise and thrill of the wide open spaces as befits all young people in the prime of their youth, Jane enjoying the freedom from the house, Daniel, with the blood coursing violently through his veins, enjoying the unaccustomed pleasure of guiding his superb mount in the attractive company of this beautiful and athletic young woman. They had reached a small moorland brook, where silver birch and hazel trees leant over a stone strewn watercourse embellished with ferns and mosses. Jane reigned in to give her horse a breather and Daniel came to rest alongside her grinning broadly. She could never remember seeing him so animated. "Help me down,

Daniel" she commanded brightly and with no more ado he dismounted and went to her horse's side to catch her, as she slid from her saddle into his arms. It was a moment of enchantment, a release of chemical stimulation so strong that it was not to be denied. As she smiled up into his face he kissed her once and then again more passionately. There was no withdrawal on her part, rather an enthusiastic response, as she kissed him back urgently until they had to part gasping for breath. Daniel stepped back totally at a loss for the words of apology, which he knew were due, but Jane, grinning mischievously up at him, spoke first. "And about time too, Daniel Robinson. I was beginning to despair that you would ever be persuaded to do that. Now kiss me again you lovely, lovely man!" He did, again and again. Soon they were lying in the heather clasping each other desperately, murmuring endearments and savouring each other's bodily presence and contact. There was no thought now of holding back, indeed no thought at all, just a release of primeval emotion and passion, their love making a joyous physical union, beautiful in its expression of love and appreciation, the one of the other. At one stage she stood outlined against the sky as she removed the last of her garments her full breasts standing provocatively proud. He, struggling to rise and kiss them, fell tangled in the ruckus of his partially removed breeches and they laughed together as they both hastened to release him. Their coupling was almost violent but exactly what they both wanted. It seemed that their passion would settle for nothing less as they rolled together over the ground, savouring each other's bodies and revelling in this blessed togetherness. The physical climax for him was totally beyond his wildest imagination. The years of repression had been totally negated and had lead to a release which left him stunned and helpless. He could only hope that things had been as good for his partner but, judging by her reaction and her loud cries of pleasure, he need not have worried. There followed a short period of peaceful immobility for both parties and then the enormity of the situation impressed itself on Daniel's mind. He rolled over and gazed into her face saying contritely

"Oh Jane, -er Miss Farlam, what can I say to 'ee. I cannot say I'm sorry for that would be an untruth; that were the most wonderful moment in my life, but what have I done to you? How can I apologise?"

She gazed steadily upon him. "Yes Daniel, you do need to apologise. You have made my backside red raw in this heather and the next time we do this it must be in a comfortable bed!"

Daniel laughed with her but his mind was grappling with the undeniable evidence of his ears. There was to be a next time! Spent as he was, he yearned even now for that next time but for the moment he gathered her into his arms and cradled her against him, speaking his thoughts as he never dared to do before.

"Jane, I have never felt this way about a woman, ever, and as you probably guessed I have never even been with a woman before. Maybe I wasn't so good this time but, like my reading, I'll get better with practice!"

Such was his mood of elation that he had produced this uncharacteristic joke and Jane, in tune with his mood, appreciated the change she had wrought in him. Turning over to look him in the eyes, she checked his monologue with her own confession.

"Daniel Robinson, you were wonderful, a real man, and just what I have yearned for. I sincerely hope this will not hurt your feelings but for me this was not the first time, as you too may have guessed. Yes, last year I had an affair with a young man, a gentleman of impeccable breeding and fortune but it was a disaster. He let me down Daniel. He let me down in the very way in which you have excelled. He was not the man you are! The experience was a total disappointment and nothing, absolutely nothing, compared with what you have given me today. I do not ask you to forgive me this lapse for it was a decision taken before I was fully aware of you as a potential lover, even though I confess that I had sized you up physically!"

She smiled at this admission and he returned the smile. Who could not in the face of this wonderful praise for his prowess as a lover? He was about to take her in his arms again when she sounded the warning of time lapsed and suggested they begin to make their way home.

Their ride home was perforce more restrained and thoughtful. Daniel had voiced his thoughts with difficulty.

"Jane my love," he began. "I am so desperately in love with you that I must needs know. Would our marriage be a complete impossibility? I have humble origins I know, I am worth nothing in worldly goods but I am strong and so very willing to work. But I think your father would balk at the prospect and I understand that but what are your own feelings? Is there any way we can overcome the difference? I do own to you that I would do anything to just be with you."

"Yes Daniel, you are right. I am sure my father would not be best pleased at the idea of our alliance; he is too much of the old school, too obsessed with the idea of station in life. And yet he is my father and we have a good deal of love between us." Jane was thinking her way through the convolutions of the situation. " I think we need time to work out our approach to him, time for him to see us together and know how suited we are for each other. A direct confrontation now would be disastrous, I'm sure, but that doesn't mean it would fail after suitable preparation. Be at peace my love, I too am very much in love and will do anything in the last resort for us to be together. It would be so much better however if it can be achieved with his blessing. You see that don't you?"

"Of course I do" he replied and added with fervour "You must know that I will do anything to prevent your unhappiness and wait as long as I must to win you for my wife."

Even as he spoke, Daniel was marvelling at the words he used. He was speaking of a possible marriage to the daughter of Richard Farlam, land owner and member of the social elite. He was speaking of a marriage to the most beautiful creature he had ever encountered, so far above him as to seem utterly unattainable, any thoughts along that line being laughingly impossible. And yet here she was, conspiring with him to bring this about! He knew that his was a lost soul. No other woman could ever replace Jane in his affections and this was not entirely physical. To be sure their sexual union had been such as to banish thoughts of any other partner being an adequate substitute but there was so much more to it than that. Her attitude to life, her almost psychic intuition as to his feelings and her sympathy for his situation would have been enough in addition to her practical common sense and direct way of approaching matters which so suited his own personality. And she was beautiful. So very lovely. Daniel, who had never been given to displays of emotion over beautiful things found himself a changed man in his ability to appreciate such virtues! He would wait for ever he told himself. And yet the promise of that 'next time' still remained uppermost in his mind. He couldn't really wait for ever!

Jane's re-entry into the Hall was not observed which was just as well given the foolish smile of which she could not rid herself. She had resolved that her father should be gradually introduced to her teaching sessions on a regular basis to see for himself how much progress Daniel was making. That is as far as his studies were concerned, she qualified with an even broader smile.

CHAPTER 4

THE FOREMAN

The weather having broken and staying bad for several weeks, had meant that Jane and Daniel had not been provided with an opportunity to repeat their physical consummation. Their regular tutorials did continue however. In fact it would have been unwise for them to alter their programme in any way, if concealment of their attraction for each other was to have been of importance, and for both of them, although for different reasons, it did seem that this was the better course of action. So their meetings continued, usually with the inhibiting presence of the grumpy, or more often somnolent old nurse, Betsy and under the benign supervision of Richard Farlam who found it occasionally pleasant to invite Daniel to a light refreshment, strictly non-alcoholic, after the lesson in order to better ascertain the level of his improvement. Jane was excluded from these meetings and so it should have been very much a man to man conversation. So it was, but not without a level of constraint which was inevitable, given the disparate social positions of the two, a fact which was noted by both from their different perspectives but not without regret in each case. There had been one glorious afternoon on a Sunday when, Richard Farlam being away on a social visit, they had taken advantage of the deep slumber into which Betsy had fallen and escaped to Jane's bedroom. For

Daniel it was an entirely new world and perhaps the surroundings or maybe the feeling of guilt associated with the occasion and the fear of discovery by the watchdog Betsy, caused him to be less able to enjoy the encounter. Jane was aware of his difficulty and appreciated the reasons for this, finding the right words to console him and encouraging him to await the advent of better weather when they could be at one, out doors and without restraint.

But all this was at the physical level and, in the absence of this degree of fulfilment, there was of necessity a broadening of knowledge of each other of a different kind. Once he had overcome his reluctance to talk about himself, Daniel found that Jane was a very sympathetic listener who did not belittle his modest aspirations but rather encouraged him to speak of them and enthused over some of his ideas about farming. She, for her part, began to appreciate a little the reason for his bitterness over the ejection of his family from the farm at High Stoupe, from the land where some of those ideas might have come to fruition. He spoke too of the fragmentation of his family, wistfully recalling some of the happier moments with them and most especially his young brother, for whom he obviously had a great affection and his face lit up as he recounted some escapade or other which they had shared. Jane gradually built up a picture of this small family and its way of life, the simplicity of which contrasted sharply with her own experiences within the social stratum she occupied. She found herself envying their sense of purpose and the ethos of working hard in order to make as decent a living as possible. Nothing could be taken for granted; everything had to be striven for and, when attained, was fully and properly appreciated. Daniel himself was not the simple character he had first appeared to be. Apart from his magnificent physique he had great strength of mind and ambition which would clearly lead him to make the most of any opportunity which came his way. Jane warmed to a man who had such undeniable self confidence, such surety of direction and purpose. This was the attitude he had displayed when he had taken her in the heather. He had wanted her, had enjoyed her without questioning the niceties of the situation. Jane revelled in the memory of that sexual experience; the power of the man to which she had yielded with a pleasure leavened with a slight frisson of fear. Such indeed was his approach to the lessons he was receiving now, tackling the project head on. For him it was a practical step to take in order to further his hopes and plans. He did not as yet appreciate the doors which could open to him in the way of accessing literature. His was a blinkered view focused entirely upon his career prospects but Jane thought that she had detected the rudiments of an interest in good writing. She hoped to exploit and broaden this for both their sakes.

To Daniel Jane was one of the mysteries of life which he could never hope to fathom. She was so far above him socially and, he thought, intellectually that there should have been no way in which their lives could have become so intertwined. And yet it had happened; she had been more than a passive partner in their love making, far from it. She had demanded as he had and been fulfilled as he had, such that he could have been in no doubt as to her reaction and her need for him. Now he was receiving other impressions. He was aware of her genuine, sympathetic interest in his affairs; her determination to hep him succeed. He was aware that her eagerness to help him with his studies transcended the mere acquisition of technique and sought to lead him on to higher things, things of which he was marginally aware even if they were of small moment compared to the pressing need to equip himself with the basic requirements to leave the world of hard labour and enter the realms of management and control. He listened to her account of her own lifestyle amongst the social elite, glimpsing facets of a totally alien world with its references to art, music and literature but was surprised to learn that it had not all been a bed of roses. He learnt of the boredom, the irritation caused by enforced association with foolish and shallow people with their aimless lives revolving around superficial trivialities. He laughed with her as she described the antics of some of the most puerile young men and could listen too without rancour as she told of her attempted love affair with one of the least obnoxious of that set. Rather than being resentful he felt somewhat superior as he heard of the physical ineptitude which the young man displayed in his attempts to provide Jane with the sexual gratification she had desired. He listened with great understanding as she spoke of the joys of the countryside, especially if one was left to explore and observe without interfering in the natural lives of their fellow creatures, and she clearly appreciated the elements and the changing weather too, whether it be benign or severe. Like Jane, he too could remember times when he had battled against the forces of nature which seemed hell bent on his destruction and had gloried in his triumph over them. Equally like Jane, he could remember occasions when nature was at its most benign and when the sweetness of the hour seemed almost unbearable. If their shared love of horses had not been enough, this appreciation of the natural world created a bond between them that was the basis of a deeper and eventually more powerful attraction. It was an attraction that was to grow and grow as they recognised the qualities each possessed whilst the winter months passed slowly by.

* * * * *

It was bitterly cold in the wind which swept down the narrow streets of Bay Town and Ruth clasped her shawl the tighter around her shoulders as she started up the hill homeward bound. The voice stopped her in her tracks. "Miss Buckram, Ruth", he called in that voice which she heard from time to time in her dreaming moments. She turned and smiled at him as he hurried over the cobbles towards her. He was clad in a thick coat over his seaman's pea jacket with a funny sort of woollen hat which covered his head, ears and a good deal of his face. He saw her smile and apologised for his bizarre appearance.

"Yes, I know I am far from fashionable but really on a November day such as this I had much rather be comfortable and warm."

Taking in her own garb which seemed to be a rather thin dress with only a shawl to cover her upper body he immediately regretted his own claim to comfort and seizing her arm he propelled her across the road and before she knew it they were entering Mrs Jackson's tea rooms. She protested even as the little bell over the door tinkled its welcome but he would have none of it.

"No, no" he insisted "it is far too cold to stand chattering outside in fact it would be our teeth that chattered mainly."

He ushered her to a chair at the window table and stilled her further protests. They were pleased to find a fire blazing in the hearth and this combined with the cheery coloured crockery and decor persuaded Jonathon to remove his outer garments including the woollen hood which he laughingly pulled off over his head.

"I bought that when we were sailing in the Baltic this summer. All the sailors wear them and I must say it is very effective at keeping the head warm. The trouble is that it frightens old ladies, children and animals – but not young ladies I'm relieved to see!"

Mrs Jackson arrived at the table and took Jonathon's order of a pot of tea and a plate of muffins. Then Jonathon, reluctant to destroy the jollity but conscious of the necessity of broaching the subject, commiserated with Ruth on the loss of her mother. She thanked him gravely but her eyes really moistened when he went on to enquire after her father.

"I'm afraid he's never been himself after mother died" she admitted. "It has somehow upset his way of thinking and he has trouble remembering things. He has had to give up his position as foreman at Highfield but Mr Farlam is letting us stay on at the farmhouse. I do the cooking and washing but father helps me out with other things".

Jonathon had heard rumours of George's affliction but had not realised that it had made him unemployable. He searched for comforting words in reply and said

"What a good thing that you can remain in the house you are used to. I would say that your father is very lucky to have you to look after him".

"Yes, he seems happy enough but it is sad to see him just pottering around when he was so active in the running of the estate. But as for staying on at the old farm, well yes, it is a great relief for me. I cannot think what a trial it would have been for him if we had had to leave. Having familiar things around him and simple tasks to do keeps him contented. He – well he doesn't seem to miss mother, in fact I don't think he realises she has gone. You know, he keeps calling me Alice and once or twice I have heard him tell people that I have left home and married a fisherman!"

Jonathon appreciated her distress and made haste to change the subject. This he did by recounting his own adventures whilst away at sea. He soon made her laugh by telling some outrageous stories of his experiences and intrigued her with descriptions of some of the ports he had visited. Adopting a more serious tone he explained that he was likely to be away at sea on a regular basis. He was working hard at obtaining his master's ticket after which he could expect to have his own command.

"But when I am in between voyages I shall be returning to Bay Town and I very much hope we might meet occasionally. I can get word to you when I shall be coming home."

Ruth was amazed that this highly educated, mature young man would actually want to seek her company. She was unaware that recent events had produced in herself a maturity, which added to her natural beauty, made her a very desirable young lady. But her amazement did not prevent her from replying quickly,

"Yes, I would like that very much indeed."

Jonathon was delighted by the ingenuous enthusiasm with which she greeted his advances. He was about to ply her with more tea when she suddenly became conscious of the passage of time and jumped to her feet.

"Oh dear" she exclaimed "I am forgetting myself. I really must get back to the farm, there is so much to do. I had been visiting Jessica, you will remember her of course, to see her new baby. A little boy, Isaac they are to call him. I was on my way home and then, well then I met you and I forgot." she finished lamely.

Jonathon laughed. "If I can make you forget your troubles and the ordinary things in life like work and duties then I have cause to be very pleased with myself."

"Yes you did do that for a while at least and I thank you for it and of course for the lovely tea and muffins, but now please excuse me, I really must go. I would like us to meet again Jonathon."

She used the name shyly, shook his hand and then hastily made for the door. As he settled the bill with Mrs Jackson and donned his cold weather gear, Jonathon was smiling in self satisfaction. He had penetrated through the shyness and reserve of this girl and made of her a friend at least. He wanted to instil more than friendship in that warm heart and admitted to himself that he was badly smitten. Of course she was far too young really; what was she? Fourteen he thought. But she was very mature for her age. Petite to be sure but strong in body and mind. She had need to be given the circumstances under which she now laboured, with a houseful of farm workers to care for as well as a dependant father, who relied upon her completely and needed watching carefully. Jonathon knew that she would blossom further in the next few years and he intended to be around when that happened and she became ripe for the marital stakes. He was determined not to miss out through inactivity on his part.

* * * * *

It was an icy January day when they told him. They had decided they must do so before Jane's condition became so obvious as to be undeniable. Incredulity was rapidly superseded by rage and, uncharacteristically for him, Richard Farlam made his fury obvious. This was not by design, not a deliberate display put on to create an effect but a genuine explosion of emotion caused by a combination of outrage, bitter disappointment and even self reproach, as he momentarily pondered on his own dereliction of duty towards a daughter, who had clearly needed protection. The interview had taken place in the study where Daniel had been wont to sit and receive his tuition from Jane. Now they all stood, rigid with the intensity of the moment as Richard Farlam, like the wrath of God, stabbed a finger towards each selected victim in turn. Jane had been the first to suffer and she stood now scarlet faced and trembling in the face of his bitter and scornful reproach. In all probability she would have been the greater affected by a 'more in sorrow than in anger' attitude on the part of her father but Richard's anger had to be expressed immediately, although the sorrow was an indisputable element of his feelings too.

Now he turned his attention to Daniel who stood pale faced but four square on to his accuser.

"And as for you, you unspeakable ingrate, is this how you repay my interest and assistance? You take advantage of my hospitality to inveigle your way into my house and then break my trust by ravishing my daughter. You doubtless schemed to procure a place in this household which would eventually lead to your becoming master of Highfield – a useful shortcut in the career of an ambitious and unscrupulous young adventurer. Well that is not what will happen. My daughter shall lose her inheritance rather than you should come to a position you do not deserve. What you do deserve is to have a horse whip put about you and by God I've a mind to see it done!"

The interruption from Jane was unlooked for and surprising in its power and vehemence. "Father, if there is to be any horse whipping you had better start with me! It is I who am responsible for this situation. I was the one who led Daniel on; I wanted it to happen. Now Daniel has asked me to marry him and I have accepted." She raised a silencing hand and continued more quietly "I would remind you that I am of age. I would have liked to receive your blessing but I will marry, with or without it and we shall accept the consequences whatever they may be." She had finished on a defiant note and the two men regarded her silently for a moment in some surprise.

It was Daniel who recovered first.

"Mr Farlam, sir, if you will give me leave to speak a few words, I cannot stand by and let Jane take all the blame like this. I know I should have found the strength to hold back but I didn't – I was so, well so swept away, I was beyond thinking straight. But it was my actions as brought this situation about so I beg you not to punish Jane. I can see how you would not want a family alliance with such as myself but I would yet say to you that given the chance I will love, honour and protect your daughter and provide and care for her as best I can."

Though Richard Farlam was to remember these words later the tide of his anger was not to be stemmed now.

"Oh you will marry the girl, that is certain, but you will not set foot in this house again. You must make shift elsewhere; there is a cottage empty in the village at this moment and I suggest you start to make your arrangements. Now you," he pointed at Daniel, "You will leave now. And you, daughter, will stay but out of my sight. I shall see you at dinner and not before."

He remained standing to oversee the departure of Daniel and Jane then slumped in his chair, head in hands, his world collapsed about him.

In the absence of instructions to the contrary, Daniel continued in his job, indeed it was necessary that he did so in order to keep the farm running. His communication with Richard Farlam was minimal and entirely confined to receiving instructions and conveying reports. In the meantime he pursued the tasks of arranging to rent the cottage in the village and also made arrangements for the wedding, which was to take place in the village church in the first week of February. The father of the bride wanted nothing whatsoever to do with this ceremony, except in as much as he wrote for and obtained a special licence for the marriage, which obviated the necessity for the reading of banns in church. Jane had busied herself with inspecting the cottage and putting together such household things as she could with ease acquire but, whilst Mary Robinson had also helped with a few items, it was clear that they would be enjoying a fairly Spartan existence. There was no hint of depression however from either of the betrothed; they were too excited at the prospect of their imminent marriage and the joy of being together in their own home.

There had been several days of hard frost with thick ice on the water troughs. The wedding, when it came, might have been expected to be a rather subdued affair. That it was not was largely due to the Robinson family and especially the attendance of young Tom, unexpectedly home from the sea at this time. Jane found him to be everything that Daniel had said of him, bright, cheerful, with a mischievous smile and a very winning way with him. She could imagine that many a foreign port would contain girls who sighed for his return and when she playfully raised this subject with him he gave her to understand that she was not too badly mistaken. The ceremony was attended by all the lads from the farm who could be spared from their work as well as the Jensons from Bay Town who had come along to give moral support to John and Mary Robinson. Everyone was aware of the circumstances which surrounded this hurried marriage, conducted in a very much more low key manner than would normally have been expected when the daughter of the local land owner was the bride. There was quite naturally a strange atmosphere caused by the absence of any member or friend of the Farlam family and people's awareness of the situation was heightened by the fact that the bride was to be given away by George Buckram. In the absence of her father, which she had wept over quietly in the privacy of her room at the Hall before she left for the last time, Jane had turned to her father's old retainer who she had known all her life and he had been delighted if baffled at being given this duty. They had left together for the church from the old farm and he had insisted that the bridal party all return there after the ceremony when, he said, Alice would be putting on a few bites of food and liquid refreshment. Folk had smiled and shaken their heads slightly at this further evidence of George's confused condition but they knew that Ruth had already been approached and was happy to prepare for their return from the church.

The actual ceremony passed without incident and the smiles on the faces of the two principals declared to the world their happiness and joy in the occasion so that, if there had been any misgivings amongst the Robinson clan, they would have been wholly dispelled. The register was duly signed, Daniel using his new found ability to inscribe his name with a proud flourish, and then the little procession formed up with the bridesmaid Naomi, Daniel's sister, following behind and George accompanying Mary Robinson, whilst John paced along beside his younger son, Tom. When they reached the porch there was a figure to meet them who removed his hat as they drew near. Jane broke away from the arm of her new husband and rushed to greet him.

"Oh father you came! I am so very glad you did." and she fell into his arms.

Richard Farlam returned her embrace and kissed her fondly. "Well I really couldn't stay away on this your wedding day my dear." He smiled sadly and then turned to a shocked and embarrassed Daniel, extending his hand. "See that you look after her Daniel, see that you do now." He donned his hat again and politely refused the invitation to attend the party in the old farm. "Forgive me but no. I have an appointment to see Dr. McClaren. We have some business to discuss partly of a professional nature and concerning yourself Jane."

He smiled at her and she blushed with pleasure at the thought that her father was now contemplating the arrival of his grandchild with apparently some happiness. With a nod to all Mr Farlam left the celebrating company and climbed into his trap, making off towards the doctor's house. That company which he had just left however was now abuzz with conjecture about the unexpected encounter. There were some knowing smiles and remarks about blood being thicker than water and those, who had conjectured that nothing good would come of such a social misalliance, began to revise their opinions. It was indeed wonderful to see the lifting of the atmosphere all brought about by that simple greeting. And yet, thought Daniel, nothing has really changed. To be sure he acknowledged me but that was for the benefit of his daughter in front of the crowd. I cannot expect forgiveness from that quarter. But it had made Jane happy and for that he was grateful.

The party in the old farm was a great success. Daniel sat there happily and mainly silently as he listened to the friendly chatter and bantering. He had made his little speech; with the experience of a few weddings in recent years he had had a good idea of what to say although there had of course been differences on this occasion. There was no father of the bride to thank but this element passed almost unnoticed in the merry atmosphere. Jane was radiantly happy as all could see and she moved constantly around the party talking naturally and cheerfully with everyone. The opinion of all was that Daniel had found himself a wonderful wife, a woman who despite her wealthy background was 'one of their own'. Jane was kept vastly amused, as indeed they all were, by the collection of yarns and anecdotes which Tom produced. Some of these stories were a bit on the ripe side but that was all right in this company and as the drink went down the tales became more risque and the laughter increased in volume. Ruth was happy in that everyone seemed to be enjoying themselves and they all complimented her upon her buffet. Daniel's parents were happy in as much as they had overcome their misgivings about what they had seen as an enforced alliance and both of them had been captivated by Jane. George was happy too and kept on telling anyone who would listen that his daughter had just married a very fine fellow and a good workman with the horses. It was late when the party broke up and the newlyweds left for their honeymoon night which had been booked at the Flask Inn on the moors: quiet, remote and ideally suited to their purposes that night. Their carriage was a specially cleaned up farm waggon; the driver Daniel himself and there were no postilions or other attendants as they set off under the clear moonlit sky with the frost shining sharply in the grass. It was bitterly cold but they had no doubts but that they would find a way to keep warm.

* * * * *

Richard Farlam meanwhile had kept his engagement with his old friend Dr McClaren and had been persuaded to stay for dinner. His purpose in going had been twofold; to receive an assurance that the good doctor would attend his daughter in her coming confinement, and to find a sympathetic ear into which he could pour his troubled feelings. McClaren was a good listener, as most successful doctors are, but the story which unfolded was in any event intriguing enough to capture his attention. The story would not perhaps have been told at all, had it not been for the loosening effect upon the tongue of the wine which had accompanied the dinner. There had been a noticeable hesitation before Richard had accepted a glass and he had apologised for his seeming rudeness. "You see Andrew, I have not touched a drop of alcohol for many years, not since I came to Highfield in fact. But I feel I could enjoy a glass now, indeed I have need of it!" He smiled as he quaffed the excellent Burgundy and complimented his host upon its quality. They discussed wines generally, the weather, the state of trade and the general economy of the country. They talked of their mutual acquaintances, their health and their follies and successes. And then finally, as the port was passed across the table, Richard spoke of himself.

He had, he told Andrew, been at a very low ebb when he first came to Highfield. As was generally known, he was a widower and had brought with him his little daughter, her nurse and his loyal foreman, George Buckram. What Andrew McClaren learned now was the background to this move and it was a sad story. Richard's father had been a high ranking official in the British Diplomatic Corps stationed in India. The family had lived there until his mother died of a fever after which father and two sons returned to England. His brother had obtained a commission in the army but Richard had opted for the life of a gentleman farmer, an occupation facilitated by the considerable financial help which his father had been able to afford him. His farm was on the Wolds near to Driffield and he had moved within circles of some social standing, becoming infatuated with the daughter of a member of the minor nobility. When his brother and father died in quick succession, the one as a result of a silly hunting accident, the other from simple old age, his greatly enhanced financial circumstances had sufficed to make him an acceptable suitor for the hand of this girl and he had married Eileen in grand style, becoming as a result a prominent member himself of the county set. They had followed a dynamic lifestyle; wining and dining, balls and garden parties, hunting and racing. Richard had followed the lead of his wife in all this, although he admitted that it had not always been quite to his taste. They had eaten well and they had drunk well. Indeed far too much of the latter, although Richard made no excuses for himself in this matter. The fact was however that Eileen, he discovered rather late, was actually becoming dependant upon her alcohol intake. There had been times when she had been incapacitated by drink in the middle of the day and on one dreadful occasion there had been a drunken altercation in front of their two year old daughter. That had ended in tears and promises to reform and there had been another pregnancy. But it had not been an easy one and Eileen had suffered greatly. The pains she endured at the end, when the child was stillborn, had been excruciating and the doctor had had to have recourse to the administration of laudanum. Eileen had persisted in the use of this drug during the long period of depression following the loss of her child and the quantities she imbibed increased gradually. To his horror Richard now perceived that she had acquired another dependency and in some anxiety he discussed matters with the doctor. That worthy agreed that it was an unfortunate situation but counselled him to have care in weaning her off the drug. He spoke of the withdrawal symptoms and suggested a gradual reduction in the amounts taken. This however was more easily proposed than achieved and the patient was certainly not above cheating, hoarding and obtaining extra supplies through friends who should have known better. It might not have been so bad if the alcohol intake had fallen but that too seemed to be increasing.

The climax came one December night when after dinner Eileen had retired to her room early. Calling on her later, Richard had discovered the room to be empty and the house was searched to no avail. The alarm was now raised and the grounds and surrounding countryside were searched by lantern light with no success. The body was found the next morning in the churchyard close to the little grave so newly furnished with a headstone. She had fallen asleep and simply frozen to death, the empty bottle by her side bespeaking the reason for her loss of consciousness.

It was a scandal of course to titillate the minds of the local populace and the tales grew the taller in the telling. Richard found himself the subject of censure for not looking after his wife properly and keeping her habits under control. Rather than sympathy, he received the cold shoulder from many of his erstwhile friends in the upper stratum of society and the invitations to their events dried up, not that he would have taken any pleasure in being in their company. He had inherited his wife's money which, in addition to his own resources born of successful farming, made him a very wealthy man. But the atmosphere in the community and the sad associations in his mind, wherever he went in house or grounds, eventually crystallised into a decision to move. He would move far away from this area in which he had become friendless and start again, taking with him his child, who he was determined would lead a life free from the evils of drink. So he had bought Highfield bringing with him his foreman, the pick of his blood stock and a style of farming more usually seen in the East Riding with its preoccupation with horses and their breeding. His money had been put to good use in the erection of a fine Hall and the building up of a splendid herd of Clydesdale horses, which were now the talk of the north of England and even Scotland. Jane had been brought up to enjoy the countryside and had naturally acquired the same passion as her father for horses, becoming a very accomplished rider.

Richard paused for a moment and regarded his friend intently. "Andrew I failed her." he said sadly. "Just like her mother, I failed her. I should have kept a close eye on things, been more conscious of the fact that she was of an age when she could fall prey to her senses." He cut short the Doctor's mild protest and continued. " I never really thought about her marriage; she had shown no inclination to take up with any of the young men we know in the area and so things just drifted along. We both seemed to be so contented. I was simply happy to have her company, hoping that it would somehow go on for ever. But, as you can imagine, if I had any thoughts about her marriage it would not have been of the sort that took place today. Like it or not, she is now tied to this young farm lad and I fear for her happiness when the physical attraction wears off and she perceives the gulf between them. Oh he is a pleasant and worthy enough young man! Industrious, conscientious and honest. I had a fondness for him myself. Still have I suppose despite what has happened." Richard was remembering now the brave stand which Daniel had taken in the face of his rage and took some comfort in his declaration of intent to look after Jane to the best of his ability. "I threw them both out you know." he admitted sorrowfully. " Told Jane she would not receive a penny from me and I wanted nothing more to do with either of them. It was the disappointment I suppose. I had wanted something better for her but now for the life of me I cannot think what." The drink was obviously now working its magic and Andrew McClaren had more sense than to interrupt his friend's flow of thought. He knew he was there as a sounding board for Richard to express his feelings without outside comment and he merely pushed the port back across the table and settled back to hear more. "It came to me very quickly afterwards, when I had recovered myself after that dreadful interview, that I had no one else to leave my money to. No family except in-laws who I would rather not see or hear from again. What else had I accumulated my wealth for if it was not for my Jane, my only daughter?" Andrew McClaren rather feared that a touch of maudlin self pity might intrude here and he would be faced with a tearful companion, which would be embarrassing to say the least, but he was wrong. Instead a smile suffused the features of Richard Farlam and he leant forward eagerly across the table. "But it's not too late is it Andrew? I can redress the situation by seeing them both tomorrow and putting things right between us. I shall withdraw my remarks, aye, even apologise for them. They shall move into the Hall, there is plenty of room, and I shall tell them both that the idea of disinheritance was a silly mistake. If the lass is happy I shall hope to keep her so. And I shall want to be a part of this new family which is coming along. At least the pair seem to be fertile enough!" and he laughed loudly at his own joke, Andrew joining in, as he was obviously expected to do.

From a fairly sombre occasion the evening was now transformed into a jolly affair and the two sat chatting amiably, or rather it was Richard who chatted of his new plans, whilst Andrew nodded in agreement or occasionally came up with a suggestion of his own. They were sitting now in front of the fire and the empty bottle had been replaced by another, there being no sign of Richard wanting to take his leave. Andrew marvelled at his guest's capacity for consuming his port but did not resent it as it had clearly had a most beneficial and therapeutic effect. But the time for departure did arrive, prompted perhaps by Andrew McClaren's repeated references to patients he had to see early on the morrow, and Richard climbed to his feet, a trifle unsteadily, thanking his friend most heartily for a wonderful evening. Andrew enquired gently if Richard felt able to undertake the drive back to Highfield but the latter smiled and confessed, "You know Andrew, I am actually redundant when I climb onto that rig. The old horse knows her way home and would manage even if I fell asleep at the reins! Not that I shall be asleep." he continued with a laugh, " My mind is full of ideas and plans for my new family."

Andrew saw him into his coat and into the trap waving him on his way and hoping that his new attitude would be well received by the young couple he had so recently alienated. He shivered in the cold air and turned back abruptly into the house.

CHAPTER 5

THE BRIDEGROOM

It was still an early breakfast despite the fact that it was the first morning of the honeymoon; necessarily so because it was a long drive back to Highfield and work must go on honeymoon or no. Even so they allowed themselves time to gaze dreamily at each other in between assailing mighty portions of cooked ham and potatoes. The hearty appetites displayed were unsurprising given the activities of the previous night. There had been of course no problem with false modesty as they arrived in their bedroom; they were too much in need of each other and no time was lost in falling into bed where they embraced passionately. Daniel's fears about the wisdom of Jane indulging in sex in her condition had been set at rest by that determined young lady and he set to with a will. Jane responded with equal passion and enjoyment. This was the man she had always secretly dreamed of; one who would take her without restraint, using the full vigour of his body to satisfy himself and her also in the process. Spent, they had lain together, he cradling her head on his chest, and they had spoken soft endearments and voiced quiet thoughts about their future. Their immediate plans centred around the creation of a suitable home in the village for themselves and their impending family but Daniel spoke of his own plans to better himself and take a tenancy on a suitable farm, hopefully in the district, but elsewhere if necessary. His ambitions were limited; it would not be another Highfield he knew and he would miss the horses but it would make for a living and a home which would suit them both. Jane smiled to herself at his enthusiasm and silently vowed to help him achieve his goals in any way she could do so. Aloud she told him how she could envisage nothing better than a life with him, raising their children and working the land. They kissed fondly and gently but the bodily contact and the intimacy of their thoughts conspired to arouse fresh waves of physical desire. They made love again and if it was less tempestuous, it was no less enjoyable and satisfying. They fell asleep in each others arms.

On the morrow the early breakfast was somewhat delayed by Daniel's determination to see his new wife properly fulfilled again but despite this they both tackled the filling meal with gusto and were preparing to take their leave, when a disturbance occurred in the yard. Glancing through the window, Daniel saw one of the grooms from Highfield leaning over a winded and sweating horse. He rose hurriedly and went out to question the lad.

"Now Jimmy, you've given that horse a hard time. I hope there's a good excuse for that!"

"Oh Mr Robinson" replied the boy. "Thank goodness I've found 'e up and about. Ye mun come back to Highfield as quick as ye can. There's bin a terrible accident."

Jane had joined them in the yard by now and had heard this last statement with some alarm.

"What is it Jimmy?" She sought the information anxiously. "Was my father involved in it?"

The lad stared at Jane and nodded awkwardly. "Aye Miss Jane – – I mean Mrs Robinson, Aye, 'e was and us all thought you'd best be comin' 'ome straight away."

Jane turned wildly to Daniel who seized her by the shoulders and said

"Right then my love. Up you get onto Jimmy's horse and set off now. Jimmy and I will be along shortly with the cart."

He helped her mount, put the reins into her hand and spoke a hurried farewell. "Take her gently lass, she's had a punishing run already this morning and her footing might not be so good."

As Jane clattered out of the yard and onto the road towards Highfield Daniel turned to the young groom and asked directly

"Now lad, 'ow bad is it then?"

"Couldn't be worse Mr Robinson" was the sad reply. "I reckon as 'ow Mr Farlam wus dead when they got 'im back to the 'all but just 'ow it 'appened I cannot tell."

Nor could the coroner. The tragic death by drowning in a mere eighteen inches of water was clearly explicable by the fact that the body had been found wedged under the overturned trap, which had somehow veered off the track at the bottom of Wrayton bank and into the beck which passed along the side of the road. What was not clear was the cause of the accident. There were obvious skid marks on the still frozen surface of the road indicating that the vehicle had slewed sideways on the bend at the bottom of the hill but, to achieve that result, the trap must have been travelling at almost runaway speed. Speculation centred around the efficiency of the brake but Alf Hodgkins the blacksmith, testified that he had personally checked the trap only a few months ago and found nothing to excite concern. The horse, which had been impaled by a broken shaft and mercifully destroyed as soon as it was found, was also the subject of some suspicion. Had it been startled by something and panicked into a fatal stampede down the hill? The grooms from the Hall all swore to the placid and reliable temperament of the animal. The intense frost and resulting glassily frozen surface of the road were clearly factors in the equation, as was the steep gradient of the bank, and on this information the verdict was reached of "accidental death precipitated by uncertain causation but with the adverse weather conditions a deciding contributory factor."

There was one of course who could have supplied a further contributory factor in this regard but Andrew McClaren held his tongue, feeling it would serve no purpose to blacken the character of his late friend. Perhaps there was also a tiny element of self interest in his reluctance to admit to sending his friend off on his return journey, in what was undeniably an alcoholic haze, but let us give the good doctor the benefit of the doubt. He really did care about the reputation of Richard Farlam, who had been a good and steadfast friend. He had testified that Richard had dined with him and left in high good spirits, having come to terms with his new circumstances as a father – in- law and prospective grandfather. He could say honestly that he had been in good health and a sound state of mind. It had been slightly difficult for him to refrain from offering the whole truth in this respect but, if the authorities had been unable to detect the degree of alcohol the deceased had taken, then he was not going to rectify the deficiency. He was helped too by Richard's well known reputation as a man with temperance inclinations. But then the die had already been cast when he had spoken to Jane and Daniel shortly after the tragedy had occurred.

At that time he had decided not to dwell upon the amount of wine and port that had been consumed but had emphasised instead the change in his attitude towards his daughter and son-in-law. "I can tell you that he was a happy man that night." he had said to them as he sat in the comfort of a big old armchair in the drawing room at Highfield. " He had told me how unreasonable he had been with you both when he learnt your news. It had been a great shock to him and I dare say" he smiled sympathetically at Daniel, " he thought it a terrible blow to his plans for his beloved daughter. But he admitted to me that when he had considered things in a cooler temper he had realised that such plans were actually quite formless. He had had no plan other than to see Jane married happily to a suitable spouse who would hopefully carry on the work at Highfield and when he thought upon this seriously he could see that you Daniel were such a man as might well bring that about. The major tragedy in my eyes is that he was unable to tell you this himself. I can only vouch for the truth of his change of attitude from our conversation at dinner and I can give you chapter and verse as to his plans! There was to be a redecoration of the guest bedroom for the two of you and the alteration of the room next door to create a directly linked nursery. There were little things too. He spoke of the joy that you Jane had had, when there was a swing hung from the biggest apple tree in the orchard, and this was to be reconstituted with immediate effect, although how a new born infant could benefit from this facility was beyond my comprehension. But do not blame him for this seemingly minor irrelevance. I was listening to a man reborn with a new interest in life. We all know about his passion for his horses but I'll warrant you he was embarking upon a new and more insistent a preoccupation – he was to be a grandfather! And there is another aspect of this tragedy – he would have been superb in that role."

* * * * *

Jane had insisted upon holding the funeral in the village church rather than going to a grander edifice in Whitby or Scarborough. As she said, those who had valued his acquaintance would be glad to make the necessary journey and accept the simple surroundings. Meanwhile the service was accessible to all the neighbourhood including the work force and all who had come into contact with him through his farming activities. That she had been quite right was proven by the tremendous turn out for the occasion. Many of the local gentry were present, as were several of those with whom he had had business dealings, including those who had purchased blood stock from him over the years, some from as far afield as Northumberland. But the vast majority of the congregation was made up of local people. Villagers, labourers, tradesmen and their wives; neighbouring farmers and their families, even the odd itinerant traveller who had occasionally sought and obtained temporary work at Highfield had all attended to show their respect for a charitable and pleasant man, a fair employer and good neighbour. Jane had been much gratified by this exhibition of the regard in which her father had been held and was at pains to greet them all and thank them for their attendance. To them all she introduced her new husband and Daniel was subjected to an embarrassing series of hand shakes, good wishes and congratulations upon his good fortune in marrying Jane. By and large he soldiered on well through this ordeal but there was one encounter which soured the entire morning. Potentially of course it was always going to be a difficult moment but his Lordship made things far worse than they might have been. Jane had noted that, when Daniel was introduced to him, His Lordship had rather looked down upon her husband and addressed him in somewhat patronising tones. Rather unwisely she was determined not to let this pass and prompted His Lordship with the ancillary information that Daniel was a member of the Robinson family, who had lost the tenancy of High Stoupe farm when the land was sold to the Alum Company. If she had expected a sympathetic word for Daniel she was to be disappointed. Instead, His Lordship after a small pause for recollection had laughed loudly and exclaimed that he had really been very fortunate over that transaction. "Damn me but those fellows were fools " he confided in them. "most expert opinion was that not only was the alum bearing shale likely to peter out but so was the market too! I think they have probably burnt their fingers badly, whilst I was able to off load a rather poor piece of land with very little earning capacity at an extremely good price." He paused to enjoy their words of approbation and congratulation only to be immersed in an icy silence, which was eventually broken by the cold but even tones of Daniel, who said that it was a pity that he and his family could not have shared in that good fortune but had been forced to seek places elsewhere. "But then," he continued, "I should think your sort never gives any thought to the futures of the poor bloody tenants," With that he turned and departed abruptly leaving a speechless peer of the realm surrounded by a shocked and horrified group of friends. No one was able to think of words to say which might have lightened the moment and His Lordship broke the tense silence with a decision to make a hasty departure, having first bidden farewell to a thoroughly embarrassed Jane. It is perhaps a pity that Daniel had not been able to unbend a little from his stance of 'the badly done by' but that was simply not in his nature, nor did it worry him that he might have ruined his chances of being received in the highest local society. Whether he did or not, the fact was that a sort of bush telegraph operated in a matter of minutes. All the visiting gentry were invited by Jane to return to Highfield Hall for refreshments and indeed many who had travelled from afar were glad to accept this offer. It was noticeable however that there was little enthusiasm from the more localised people of quality who followed the lead of his Lordship in declining with murmured words of thanks.

It was but a small party then which gathered in the Hall and, because of the distances involved and the time of the year, most of the guests made an early departure. Daniel was sorry to see them go. They were all people of his own disposition, lovers of horses even if they were primarily dealers and businessmen. He had felt a kinship based even upon this slight acquaintance and was ready and anxious to continue to do business with them. Finally only Andrew McClaren was left and eventually he too rose to make his departure. As he did so, he embraced Jane and wished her well in the future and then turning to Daniel he put an arm on his shoulder and said

"Well my boy, you're in charge of Highfield now and I do not doubt but that you'll make an excellent job of it. Bye the bye I would very much like to carry out my friend's last wishes and attend Jane in her confinement – that is if you have no objections?"

He smiled hopefully at them and was rewarded with warm and grateful thanks. Andrew McClaren was one member of the gentry who stood well in Daniel's regard. Daniel saw him into his coat and watched him drive away down the road from the Hall then stayed on the steps to survey the land in the dying light of the winter's afternoon. Andrew's words were repeating themselves in his ear. He was in charge now! It seemed but a short time ago that he had first come to the estate as a slightly apprehensive, if willing, horse lad. The past few years had seen a most remarkable change in his fortunes and the pace of that change had accelerated at a rate which often left him bewildered. But bewildered or not, the fact remained that he was now in charge. Albeit by virtue of his wife's ownership, he, Daniel Robinson, was Master of Highfield!

CHAPTER 6

THE MASTER

The Master of Highfield leant contentedly in his customary position against the yard gate, arms lying on the top bar and chin resting on his joined hands, as he surveyed his realm down to the cliff tops and indeed beyond, to where a wheeling flock of gulls announced the gutting of the catch on the inward bound cobble. Those gulls shone brilliantly white in the low rays of the evening sun and, even at this distance, he fancied he could detect the tiny flashes of foam as the otherwise limpid water was turned over by the heavy oars of the boat. There was not a breath of wind, unusual for this coast, and so the tiny sounds of the evening, a bleating lamb, a calling curlew, melded with the sharply delineated beauty of the pastoral scene to create an atmosphere of total peace and tranquillity. It was a time for contemplation and reflection rather than a practical appraisal of crops and animals and Daniel was indulging himself to the full in this exercise.

There was certainly cause for satisfaction; his marriage for example. Their relationship, based initially upon the heady passion born of their mutual strong physical attraction, had broadened into something much deeper and more lasting. There had been a growing intimacy of the mind, an increase in understanding and appreciation, which had clearly enriched their lives. Not that the physical element had diminished – far from it as was evidenced by the arrival of the two children with a third on the way. Those children, first Mary and then little Richard, had brought them even closer together. Daniel's working day was such as to prevent him being able to spend much time with them but he was very fond of them both and as proud of his family as any of his achievements on the estate. Their care remained firmly in the domain of Jane of course, as was right and proper, and she tried to ensure, as was also right and proper, that their father was not troubled by noisy, demanding children when he came in from his long, hard day in the fields. But the truth was that he loved to come in for his share of attention from those lively sprites, no matter how exhausted he felt. The impending arrival of another squalling child would ensure a loss of sleep he could ill afford but he had lived through all that before and was quite looking forward to the new arrival. Right on cue there came a wail of protest from the Hall cut sharply short and not repeated. Daniel grinned. Devoted though she was to them, Jane stood for no nonsense and ran them with a tight rein. Soon he would have to go into the house and assume the role of gruff but amiable father, a role which came entirely naturally to him.

In the bathroom Jane patted little Richard dry whilst the maid, Lizzie, rubbed down Mary; it was the latter who had protested against her removal from the warm water. Jane guessed that cry would have been heard, knew exactly where Daniel would be at this time and smiled quietly to herself as she anticipated his arrival back in the house perfectly timed to greet his shiningly clean offspring as they descended from the bathroom. She always relished this time when her husband allowed himself, with some counterfeit show of reluctance, to enter into a game usually vigorous and exciting with the two before they were whisked off to bed, where a quiet story from Jane settled them down for sleep.

Jane knew that Daniel would indeed be tired after his long and arduous day. He was gluttonous in his desire for punishment, as far as work and responsibility for the farm was concerned. He worked in the capacity of both owner and foreman, throwing himself into any task which he felt demanded his help and example. He drove his men hard but they had little cause for complaint when their master worked as hard as themselves. He might have had an even harder time of it, had she not eventually persuaded him that, with all the help she had in the house, she could take on the management of the horse breeding programme and the handling of sales and purchases of stock. She dealt with all kinds of buyers from farmers seeking good ploughing and general working animals, to businesses requiring strong teams of horses to pull their heavy trucks and carts. Recently there had been a useful breakthrough into the market for brewery dray horses, not merely the local firms of Russells and Roses in Malton, but bigger concerns from further afield in Tadcaster and Leeds. Recently, with the loss of some household staff and the demands of the growing children, she had been finding it more difficult and she resolved to ask Daniel again if she could take on another helper.

Once he had become accustomed to the idea of Jane handling this side of the farm management, Daniel had been amused by it. He rightly guessed that the dealers would be eager to do business with a woman who, ladylike and refined, would clearly be no match for them in the process of haggling over prices, even if it were conceded that she was quite knowledgeable as far as the quality of the horses was concerned. All they had to do was to ensure that the husband was well out of earshot as the bargaining went on but they little realised that Daniel was more than content to leave this all to his shrewd and calculating wife. Many a dealer would shake his head in disbelief as he rode away having paid more for his acquisitions than he had even remotely anticipated. But it was all done with a smile, good humour and the production of hearty refreshment after the deal was concluded so that the victim could still return home in a happy frame of mind, whilst vowing not to be so badly taken in next time.

All in all it was a splendid combination, the skills and propensities of each complementing those of the other. As Jane once said to him "An ideal working arrangement my dearest love." And yes, she frequently addressed him in this shamelessly sentimental fashion, when the most she could expect in return was the very occasional "Tha's a grand lass Jane." But Jane could remember the little deeds which took the place of words; the tray of tea and muffins adorned with a trailing sprig of honeysuckle, which arrived at her bedside when she was lying in after the birth of Richard, the egg cup tightly filled with primroses awaiting her on the breakfast table when she came down after he had gone out to work. Not all the time of course. Not even very often to be honest, but just now and then a little touch to thrill her with the knowledge that he cared.

As usual supper was to be eaten in the kitchen on the large table which adapted itself so well to family use. The dining room was used seldom used these days, being reserved for the very infrequent formal occasions or the entertainment of visiting buyers. Whilst happy enough in the cosy atmosphere of the workaday kitchen, Jane did experience the occasional twinge of regret at the passing of the days, when a glittering company might be assembled in the formal rooms of the big house, when the wine and conversation flowed and the latest fashions were proudly displayed. But these social occasions simply did not occur any more. Ever since the unfortunate encounter with His Lordship at the funeral of Richard Farlam, the Robinsons of Highfield had become somewhat off limits for those who considered themselves to be the upper classes of the area. True there were exceptions; Dr McClaren remained a good friend and was always welcome at a Highfield which had become rather more welcoming in terms of its provision of suitable liquid refreshment for the visitor. Daniel got on well with the good doctor, had cause to be grateful for the care he had lavished upon Jane, and, having discovered his predilection for a glass of spirit now and again, had made sure that there was always a supply in the study cabinet. In latter years he had himself been persuaded to take a drink but always in the greatest moderation. Despite Andrew's lack of specialist knowledge on the subject, he was nevertheless the one person with whom Daniel would discuss his ideas and plans for the estate. As well as being used as a sounding board, Andrew's opinions on matters other than farming were listened to with great attention and respect.

For his part, Andrew McClaren had an equal respect for his young friend and a sympathetic understanding of his position. He could imagine for example how difficult the sudden transition from hired hand to Master of Highfield had been for him in terms of his relationship with the work force. These were his sort of people, the folk with whom he should have been most in touch, the very substance of his background and upbringing. Now all that had changed and an unbridgeable gulf had opened between he and them. Jane had told him of how, although they spoke the same language, the camaraderie between Daniel and the horse lads had all but disappeared and, when he chanced by, their cheerful chattering usually gave way to a respectful silence. Andrew McClaren could well believe that, in view of his self imposed estrangement from the land owning classes, Daniel would feel to be neither flesh, fish nor fowl.

Whilst Daniel was up in the bathroom divesting himself of clothes pervaded with the air of barn and stable, Jane was attending to the production of supper. Lizzie was setting the table and Jane noted with annoyance that, as so frequently seemed to be the case, her hands were very grubby and her fingernails quite black. As she had done on innumerable occasions in the past, Jane pulled the girl up sharply giving her a good dressing down and sending her into the scullery to scrub her hands, which hands were duly inspected carefully on her return. All of this Lizzie submitted to with a vacuous smile and an attitude of indifference, which prompted Jane yet again to conclude that the girl was grossly lacking in intelligence as well as decent standards of cleanliness. Being the only local girl available at the time, Lizzie had replaced Jane's old nurse, Betsy, who had died just a few months after the birth of Richard. Jane thought fondly of old Betsy, who had been her nurse from the day of her birth and who, along with George Buckram, had accompanied the family on its move from the Wolds. She experienced a moment of misgiving at the thought of being attended by this dubious creature in her coming confinement but gave a mental shrug and admitted to herself that at least Lizzie was quiet and biddable. In any case, there was no substitute to be had and Jane dwelt for a while on her perception as to why this was the case.

There had been a slow but steady depletion of servants over the last few years as a result of births, marriages and deaths, the former being a totally unexpected event, unsuspected by all in the household until a matter of hours before it occurred. The deficiencies had not been rectified, partly because the new lifestyle of Highfield did not require the same number of servants, and partly because they did not seem to want to come and work at the Hall. Jane was convinced that this reluctance was due to a fear of her husband, or at least a fear of his reputation as a hard task master and she had to concede that this reputation was not ill-founded. The grooms were kept on to care for the breeding mares and also the riding horses for she and Daniel still enjoyed to ride together in the country when work allowed.

Once he had taken her to the site of his old home, High Stoupe farm, and they had gazed at the forlorn and derelict buildings. The predictors of failure had been right in their assertion that the company had made a mistake. Only a few years after taking over this new site, they had gone out of business. New methods of producing sulphuric acid meant that alum could be synthesised much more cheaply than in its laborious extraction from shale. They could not compete and so they closed down. Indeed, with the closure of the Kettleness works shortly afterwards, there had come to an end some two centuries of the alum mining trade on the Yorkshire coast. But the evidence of their activities was still to be seen. Together they rode down to the beach level and Daniel pointed out the channels which had been laboriously cut into the rock to allow ships to discharge their cargo of urine, brought from Newcastle and Sunderland, and return with a load of alum. Jane thought he was joking until he explained that the urine was a cheap source of ammonia necessary to the production of the alum salt. There were still the remains of the alum houses, where the salts had been heated in great pans, but all was now in decay and clearly suffering from the effects of weather.

Throughout this survey of his old haunts Jane noted that there was merely a slight wistfulness in his gaze and apparently none of the anger which he had once felt. Jane realised that, although he was not consciously aware of it, he had transferred all his passion for the old farmstead of his boyhood into a driving ambition to make a success of the Highfield estate. She understood this, as she understood that his single minded obsession with the economical running of the farm was intended for the good of herself and the family, but the steely way in which he pursued this end often disturbed her. For the most part, the men and boys all needed the work desperately so they were prepared to accept the tough regime, the more so because they were at least treated fairly and the horse lads in particular were appreciative of the excellent food and accommodation provided in the old farm house, run by the cheerfully efficient young Ruth. It was actually this aspect of the farm life which had given rise to the only trouble which had ever arisen between Jane and Daniel.

As rows go it was brief but of an incandescent intensity. It commenced with Daniel's casual announcement that he had found a new hind. Walter Simpson would assume the job of foreman and his wife Sally would look after the catering and housing of the horse lads. Jane had been appalled.

"But Daniel," she had protested, "what on earth are you thinking about? Where do you think the Buckrams will be able to go and how do you imagine they will be able to live? I know she is very young but Ruth has been making a wonderful job of looking after the lads and has taken on all the tasks which Alice used to do."

"Aye, I know that lass, Ruth does well enough but old George is worse than useless now and we could do with having a proper foreman, who can pull his weight on't job. If we get rid of them both the old farm becomes vacant for a suitable couple. It's a matter of greater economy lass."

There was a few moments of pregnant silence and then Jane gave her husband the benefit of a tongue lashing which completely stunned him. She denounced him as an unfeeling old miser, and in a mounting fury she pointed out that George had been a loyal and valued old retainer, having served the family well over its years both in the east Riding and now here. She reminded Daniel of the friendly reception given to him by George, when he had first arrived at Highfield, and the help and support he had given him in his days as a horse lad.

"I just cannot believe my ears Daniel! I cannot think that you would do such a monstrous thing to a man who befriended you so, and looked out for you when you first came to Highfield. You were full of praise for him then I remember; looked up to him as a teacher and exemplar and now you want to throw him on the scrap heap!"

Daniel was not sure what an exemplar was, but he did realise that he had greatly upset his wife and made a feeble attempt to further justify his suggestion by claiming that it had just been an idea to increase efficiency. It was a mistake. Positively shaking with rage now Jane shouted at him

"Efficiency! Efficiency! Is that all you can think of? Does not loyalty and gratitude have a place in your heart or does nothing but money count? Well that is not the way my mind works. Let me remind you Daniel Robinson that it was George Buckram who came with me and my father from Driffield and helped to make this place in to the fine estate it is today! It was George Buckram who helped to look after me as a little girl and I am not going to forget that on the grounds of 'efficiency'. And it seems I must also needs remind you, Daniel Robinson, that my father left this estate to me! It is I who am the real legal owner of Highfield and there is no way in which I will ever agree to dispensing with the services of the Buckrams!"

Spent now, she felt some of the resolution draining from her but maintained her posture and the fierce gaze she had fixed upon her husband. With a touch of alarm she watched the blackening of his countenance as he absorbed this final sally, but without a word he had turned and stalked out of the room. She knew she had hurt him with this reminder of his true status but was unrepentant in view of what she saw as the enormity of his unfeeling attitude.

That had been many months ago. The subject had never been referred to again and the Buckram family remained in situ in the old farm house. It seemed to Jane that Daniel had put the idea right out of his mind. He had not.

* * * * *

Totally unaware of the argument which had raged over her continued incumbency of the old farm house, Ruth carried on her task as hind to the several young horse lads and did so with some enthusiasm. There was certainly plenty to keep her occupied: cooking and baking, washing and ironing, sewing and mending, cleaning and tidying all in addition to running the home farm. She looked after the poultry, collected milk from the dairy, separated it and made butter and cheeses, all of which she had learnt from her mother. Alice had taught her well and after her death the running of the household had continued almost seamlessly so that all was as it had been before. Except for George of course.

He was now proving to be an additional source of worry and responsibility for his young daughter. His mental condition had in fact deteriorated over the last few years and now he spoke to Ruth and friends of long standing as though they were complete strangers. He pottered about the farm, often being found in the tack room examining horse collars or bridles. He would appear from the granary with an enamel cup full of corn but, when asked whither it was bound, would be unable to explain. Occasionally items of farm equipment, hay rakes or shears, would disappear and turn up again in odd places but apart from these mild nuisances he largely kept out of everyone's way and caused no real trouble. On sunny days he might be found sitting in the yard whittling away at some piece of wood but, whatever the original intention had been, no final product ever materialised. Ruth had no real cause to worry seriously about him; he ate well, slept well and was usually content to follow her directions silently with a seraphic, almost otherworldly smile on his face. But whilst young girls are not usually given to contemplating their mortality, death had touched Ruth's life several times in recent years and that made her conscious of the dangers of her father's situation. She was confident that, as long as she was with him, he would be all right but she shuddered to think of what might happen to him if she were no longer around. If anything happened to her it would probably mean the lunatic asylum in Scarborough for George and the horrific rumours, which circulated about the conditions obtaining within those walls, terrified her.

Today however those sombre thoughts were behind her, as she made her regular shopping trip into Bay Town. This was always enjoyable, much more so than her infrequent visits to Whitby, for here she knew many people and was known by them. There was always the business of gathering local news from the friendly proprietors of the little village stores, the chance encounters in the narrow streets with acquaintances, with whom one could exchange gossip and refresh family histories; all in all a wonderful feeling of belonging even as a peripheral member of the community and of course, as such, she was herself a source of information on all the goings on at Highfield. After the serious business of shopping there was then the pleasure of calling upon Aunt Martha and Uncle Jethro, where there was always a warm welcome and a hot meal which was traditionally pressed upon her despite her earlier protests. They too found her visits a great pleasure especially now that Simeon, as well as Jessica, was married and living away from home. There was always much to talk about and today the subject which dominated the conversation was the so called scandal of the failure of the lifeboat to turn out for a rescue during the past week. In the event the Whitby boat had been able to deal with the situation and the knowledge that this was possible had probably influenced the decision of the local crew not to put to sea. All the fishermen agreed that the Bay Town boat was in a dreadful condition and had not been used since its last rescue mission ten years earlier. There were some who went as far as saying she was a death trap and Uncle Jethro went along with this assessment. He was nonetheless upset by the inevitable charges of cowardice made by people who should have known better and it was certainly a great consolation to have heard of the remarks made by the Whitby Coxwain to the effect that it had been a sensible decision and he for one would not have set foot in the Bay Town boat. But there had been a definite bruising of the pride of the local inhabitants and the subject had monopolised the talk in the 'King's Head' all week with many raised voices and not a few raised fists so that the landlady, Mrs Anderson, had banned the topic and refused to serve anyone who broke the rule. Talk reverted to family matters and the impending increase in its numbers before touching upon Ruth's current situation. Naturally she was quizzed, and of course teased by Jethro, about her life on the farm. There had been the suggestion that, with all those horse lads to choose from, she would be joining the ranks of the maritally blessed before long but she explained that she had made it plain to all the men in her household that she was walking out with her own beau. From various outside sources they had been given to understand that he was a fine catch for her but, as none of them had actually encountered this prodigy, they were unable to gauge the truth of this assertion. This association of their niece with Jonathon Stormson had exercised the thoughts and concerns of the Jensens for some time and once again they questioned her as to his intentions. Ruth explained yet again that he was working for his master's ticket and could not consider marriage until he had succeeded. She was content to wait, she said, until everything was right but Martha detected a slightly false note in this seemingly confident explanation and drew her aside after the meal for a 'woman to woman chat'. Under pressure Ruth did admit that she was finding the long wait tiresome and hoped that Jonathon would soon make a serious offer and set a date. She told her aunt that he had explained to her that he wanted to wait until he was properly qualified and could afford to buy his own house. His aunt Greta he said, being a very private and fastidious old lady, would not countenance the idea of them, or indeed anyone else, living in her house. Martha nodded her head but thought privately that any young man worth his salt, and with serious intentions, would have found some quicker way to go about the job of marrying his sweetheart. Young people are always happier to tie the knot and be together even if it means accepting difficult living conditions for a while. Although it might be said that he was thinking of the comfort of his intended bride, Mr Stormson sounded to be altogether too particular and she could not help but wonder as to the strength of his commitment to her niece.

In fact Ruth too was a little unhappy about the situation. She had of course accepted his explanations about the desirability of his being able to set up house properly when he married but she had noticed a strange and unsettling thing about his discussion of the future. Quite frequently it sounded entirely impersonal, an academic exercise in fact with little of the warmth and excitement which she felt herself at the prospect. He was always so courteous and considerate on their outings together, which she thoroughly enjoyed. His greeting was always affectionate and included a kiss on the cheek – a little peck and no more she thought regretfully. But that was where it seemed to end. She recalled again the occasion when, walking through the woods surrounding the beck, she had insisted upon climbing a tree to inspect a possible woodpecker's nest. Having failed to find any sign of the bird she descended quickly, slipping down the last few feet into his arms. As he caught her, his hand involuntarily cupped her breast and she relived again that delicious feeling. He, however, snatched his hand away and, with slightly reddened countenance, launched into a discussion of the nesting habits of various woodland birds. Clearly he had been highly embarrassed by the incident and clearly Ruth realised that she would be in no danger of him ever trying to go too far. She would be quite safe with Jonathon. But Ruth was not sure that she wanted to be that safe. Was he not physically attracted to her? She had watched her employer's family grow, had enjoyed the occasional visits they made to the farm when Jane collected some eggs or butter with Richard exploring every corner of the old kitchen and Mary asking endless questions about the baking or other housework which was going on at the time. Although no mention had been made of it, she was sure too that there would be a third child in a few months. Jessica was now the mother of two and Ruth was Godmother to one of them. Simeon was married and there was a child on the way. Surrounded by all this fecundity, it was not surprising that sometimes Ruth thought that life was passing her by. There was another rather more insidiously worrying factor in her romance. Until recently they had most frequently gone out as a twosome but one Sunday afternoon Jonathon had persuaded her to attend a tea party given by one of his friends at her parents residence 'above town', where there would be some musical entertainment. Somewhat nervously she had put on her best dress and accompanied him to the splendid house overlooking the bay. Her worst apprehensions were realised. Amongst the smart and fashionable young ladies she felt gauche and out of place. Whilst she enjoyed the music, she found the conversation excruciating. She had little in common with the rest of the company, did not share any acquaintances with them other than Jonathon and was completely lost in the discussions on art and literature, about which everyone else there seemed to be an expert. Ruth could not help but wonder if her future husband would quickly tire of his unsophisticated wife. But she had faith and knew that it would all work out in the end could, she but be patient.

It was a faith that was to be tested shortly after this event. On a rare visit to Whitby one Saturday, she had espied a young lady with the flaming red hair which had made such an impression on her at the tea party. She was being handed down from a carriage by a young man who had his back to her. That did not prevent her instant identification of him as Jonathon and she watched in horrid fascination as, laughing together, the couple strolled down the street and up the steps into the 'George'. At their next meeting she lost no time in telling Jonathon that she had observed him with this girl and he, after only the briefest of embarrassed silences, had explained that she was the daughter of a ship owner who had promised him a command once he had his ticket. It was of course necessary to keep well in with the family and to socialise as and when required. Ruth had accepted this as a true and natural explanation of affairs. It did nothing however to lessen her feeling of inadequacy in terms of matching his social and cultural status but Ruth felt that she could perhaps improve her situation by a determined effort of self education. After all Daniel Robinson had done so hadn't he? And just look how happy that couple were! How she yearned for a similar happiness.

* * * * *

Between the bouts of feverish insensibility there came a lucid moment and Jane suspected that it might well be her last.

"Daniel my love" she whispered.

"Aye lass, I'm here" was the immediate reply.

"Daniel I need to speak with you. You know that I must be leaving you soon."

"Nay lass! Don't talk that way. We shall fight against it together and bring you safe through."

He squeezed her hand as though the very pressure might prevent her life from slipping away. She gave a wan smile of denial and he thought his heart would break as he gazed into those fever bright eyes. She had feebly placed a finger over his lips to still his protestations.

"Now Daniel, you know t'is so, we both do, so listen to me my dearest. Do not fret for me; I should be dying a happy woman after all our fine times together and with all the love you have given to me."

Aye, but once too often he thought with bitter self recrimination.

"And yet I am loath to leave you and the children." She breathed the words almost silently. "Oh, the children!" she repeated with more urgency, "our dear children. Promise me my darling that you will look after our children, for my sake, for my memory."

Once again he squeezed her hand. "Wye now of course lass" he assured her with all the power he could muster but in the knowledge that, although she would never know it, he was already failing her in this respect. The newly born little girl, who lay in the crib next door, was already succumbing to the same puerperal fever that was killing the mother and less than an hour ago Andrew McClaren had shaken his head sadly over both his patients and declared that they were in the hands of God.

He saw her body relax and only just heard the last request.

"Then hold me my love, hold me just one more time."

As she felt the powerful but gentle hands embrace her, and the tiny drops of moisture fall upon her face, Jane's last thought was one of astonishment. For the first time in all the years she had known him, her strong and silent husband, the stern and hard Daniel Robinson, was weeping! It was almost worth dying for! And the hint of a smile, which this thought brought to her lips, remained frozen there as she passed gently away.

Chapter 7

The Arrangement

It was raining hard as he crossed the yard and he grunted in annoyance, as he stepped into a pile of horse manure and skidded wildly before recovering his balance. By God but some lad would pay for that! Reaching the door of the wash house, he stood out in the rain whilst he used the yard brush to remove the offending material from his boots. It was always raining these days or so it seemed. The dull skies and cheerless outlook suited his mood as he clumped indoors and discarded his boots and oilskin onto the washroom floor. He marched in stockinged feet into the dining room cum office, where he rummaged about to find the last account from the forage merchant. He wanted to study that against his own records for he suspected that, either he was being overcharged deliberately, or there had been some error. Jane would have been able to spot any discrepancy in an instant. By God but how he missed her! He stared unseeingly at the paper in his hand, as he relived the events of the past few months. He had not intended that the funeral be a grand affair but then one has no control over the number of people who wish to pay their last respects on such an occasion. He had been astonished at the numbers who had turned up at the church. It had been raining on that day too he remembered and it had seemed fit and proper that it do so.

Daniel didn't know whether to feel irritated or gratified at the number of carriages arrayed outside the churchyard wall. The quality had turned out in numbers; people who he had not seen nor heard from since the day of Richard Farlam's funeral. He realised that of course he was witnessing the upper classes paying tribute to one of their own and that Jane and her father had enjoyed the friendship and respect of many such people, before he had come onto the scene. Just for a moment he had experienced a twinge of regret that he had by his attitude and behaviour estranged his wife from this company thus removing from her life an element of social contact which she had probably missed.

There were many others present too; dealers and representatives of firms with whom they had done business were in attendance and these he himself knew well, receiving their condolences and handshakes with a quiet word of thanks. And then came a moment which he had been dreading. As he stood gazing down into the open grave with an uncomprehending child on each hand, his Lordship had approached and addressed him.

"Mr Robinson, please allow me to offer my condolences on the loss of your lovely wife, a fine woman; a great loss to you I'm sure but also a loss to all in the community, where she was so well regarded. Will you take my hand sir? It is offered in all sincerity and with much sympathy."

Startled, Daniel looked into the eyes of the man he thought he had cause to detest and found nothing there but sorrow and friendly sympathy. He took the proffered hand and said

"I do thank you for that my Lord and for attending today. I would be pleased if, when we leave, you could come back to the Hall where there is a cold spread."

He had nearly used the word 'collation' but was not sure if it was correct and did not want to spoil the moment with a silly gaffe. His Lordship had smiled and gently shaken his head.

"Kind of you, Mr Robinson, very kind and I am genuinely sorry that I must decline on this occasion. I can only hope that there will be a happier one some time when perhaps I might be invited again."

He raised his hat and was about to leave when he stopped and turned back.

"You have two very fine children Mr Robinson, a well set up little boy and a young lady who will bid fair to outshining all the other beauties in the district. I hope it will be a consoling thought for you that Jane will live on for you through those children. Yes, I do hope so".

Then he departed, leaving a thoughtful Daniel to his grief.

That had been over three months ago, three months in which to get over his loss; but of course he hadn't. His mother had stayed at the Hall for nearly three weeks to help him reorganise his life and oversee the welfare of her grandchildren, during the difficult days of their gradual realisation of the permanence of their loss. He had been very grateful for her help and sorry to see her depart for her home again but he understood well enough that she needed to be back to look after his father, who these days was not getting about too well. There was also another important reason for her to return – the impending wedding of his sister. Naomi was engaged to a young man from Whitby, who was employed in a shipbuilding yard, a nice enough lad named Peter Burns who was an excellent carpenter and likely to be a useful husband when it came to jobs in the house. One really cheering piece of news was that Tom was going to be able to attend, his period of leave coinciding nicely with events in Yorkshire. Daniel was certainly looking forward to a reunion with his brother.

Mary Robinson had worked hard during her few weeks of custody of Highfield Hall. Under her direction, and in fact with her active participation, each and every room had been thoroughly spring cleaned, carpets and furniture cleaned, curtains washed, windows polished everything set in order. She had born down hard on Lizzie, who she thought to be an idle girl and, from the state of the house, not too cleanly either, but when she had mentioned this to Daniel he had sighed and shaken his head saying

"Aye mother, ah know she's not too bright but she manages to put t'food on't table and care for't bairns. In any case there is no other lass available from t'village."

"Well I should start looking further afield Daniel 'cos I reckon as 'ow she'll be letting you down badly one of these days" was the grim reply.

She repeated this warning on the day she left but Daniel was too taken up with the state of his larder to think about it seriously. The ovens had been put to good use and loaves of fresh bread had been baked along with apple pies and some of Mary's wonderful cakes including most especially her 'maids of honour' for which she was renowned in the locality. The crowning gift however had been a large tin full of his favourite shortbread biscuits and he had resolved to make them last as long as possible. Alas he was never very good at keeping to that sort of resolution.

With his mother's departure, Daniel threw himself back into work, hoping to drown his unhappiness in exhaustion. He was however always conscious of the need to reserve some time for his little ones. The midday meal was still taken in the kitchen and was usually a noisy affair with the children vying for his attention. Demanding though it was, he always felt renewed when he went back out for the afternoon's work. In the evening he had taken to using the dining room again, wanting a little privacy to deal with his paperwork. The children were admitted after their supper for a half hour or so and the family were very much at one on these occasions. It was on one such evening that he had had to answer the long dreaded questions, put to him by Mary in a very straightforward fashion.

"Mummy is really dead isn't she Daddy?"

"Yes my love she is."

"That means she isn't ever going to come back again doesn't it?"

"Aye my darling it does. And it means that we three have to look after each other, and love each other all the more, doesn't it?"

There was a pause whilst this was digested; then "When you die Daddy, what will happen to us? I don't think I'm big enough to look after Richard."

Daniel had to assure them that there was no chance of his passing away for many, many years by which time they would both be grown up and able to look after themselves. There was a sigh followed by

"That's all right then Daddy but it would be better if you didn't die at all."

Wordlessly, Daniel had drawn them both to him and cuddled them closely.

Throwing himself into his work was all right and did something to alleviate the terrible feeling of despair at the loss of Jane, who he knew was the only woman he would ever love, but it was not the solution to everything. He knew he should be devoting more time to the house and his children, had not forgotten the advice from his mother about the unsuitability of Lizzie but he had yet to face up to that problem. Even Andrew McClaren had hinted at his concern about the Hall and its servant. The good doctor still came to visit and Daniel was both pleased and relieved that this was the case. They would sit for hours in the dining room after a meal and do some justice to a bottle of brandy with plenty of serious conversation, so that Dr McClaren was reminded of the good old days when he conversed with his old friend Richard Farlam. The only difference was that his host was much younger than he, much less experienced in the ways of the world of culture and business, but happily much more liberal in his supply of good liquor. The thing about Daniel which impressed Andrew McClaren so much was his willingness to listen and to accept counselling. As a successful farmer, he had every right to assume an attitude of complacency and rebuff any proffered advice as unnecessary but he did not. He listened attentively and asked pertinent questions throughout their long talks. Andrew certainly liked to think that his advice and suggestions were heeded and benefited the man and his estate. Perhaps the secret of his success in capturing Daniel's willingness to listen was due to the fact that he managed to convey the impression that most of the possible projects emanating from their talks had been Daniel's ideas. Whatever the truth of that, both men enjoyed their discourse and the accompanying beverages. Recently Daniel had been surprised at the amount of brandy or whisky he had had to buy to sustain their evenings pleasure and at one time his suspicions had been aroused to the extent that he had marked the levels on the bottles but subsequent examinations had shown no diminution in the volume of the contents in between their social evenings.

Andrew had only hesitantly mentioned his concerns about the servant Lizzie and then only in very general terms. He certainly kept under his hat the suspicion that had remained in his mind as to the part she may have played in the death of Jane. He was one of those doctors who subscribed to modern theories that lack of cleanliness was a direct cause of many infections but there was no proof and no more justification for action other than a general distaste for her slovenliness. Daniel listened but seemed not to take the matter too seriously so that Andrew was resigned to her continued position at the Hall. In the event her downfall was not due to her lack of hygiene but for another reason altogether. Medical advisor though Andrew may have been, there was one topic, one area of needed advice which Daniel avoided in these conversations. He missed Jane dreadfully; missed her bright conversation, her constant helpfulness her competence as well as her love and companionship. One other thing, a major item, which he sadly missed was the sex they had enjoyed together, so unrestrainedly, and so mutually satisfying. In the early days, he had told himself that no woman could take the place of Jane; no female could attract him sexually ever again. If the former was true however, the latter was not. It had been in early October, on a pleasant sunny afernoon that he had been walking his fields down by the cliff edge. There had been a movement which had caught his eye and going to investigate he came across a young couple who were clearly in the throes of a passionate sexual encounter. It was several seconds before he was able to tear his gaze from the scene but, when he turned and moved quietly away, he was more disturbed than shocked. The encounter had brought back memories of similar al fresco unions with his beloved Jane and he was surprised and disgusted by his own arousal and hurried away in shame and some discomfiture. But the truth could not be blinked. He had experienced a moment of desire and he knew that desire would be a permanent part of his existence. His sexual appetite was really undimmed and as such it was entirely separated from the love he still felt for his deceased wife. This incident had merely brought into the open a feeling of deprivation which had existed in his subconscious for some time. Now that this deprivation had been acknowledged by his conscious mind, he was tortured by a feeling of disloyalty to his wife, so recently taken from him, but that did not dispel the need for relief which grew rather than diminished as time went by.

* * * * *

He knew it was a mistake as he stepped through the door which opened from the mean little street below the castle ramparts in Scarborough. The room he entered was both dingy and dirty. The very dimmest of glows was discernable from the little piles of sea coal in the grate and only one small oil lamp cast a light on the sparse furniture, which included a crib tucked under the stairs. Daniel looked about him in dismay and stared again at the girl who had brought him here. She had passably good looking features and an undeniably voluptuous figure draped in clothes of a garish hue and which had seen better days. She had been one of the better ones who had offered themselves as he strolled through the town, an obvious potential customer to the girls on the game. But the thing which put him off totally was the smell. It was a smell compounded of unwashed bodies and dirty linen, decaying food and stale beer with not a hint of fresh air being admitted to clear the stench. Like most men of his background, Daniel was not overly fastidious but this was too much for him. The girl was insistently trying to get him to remove his coat but he was already backing off and turning for the door. With a muttered apology he placed a shilling in the girl's hand and dived out into the street leaving the sniggering woman gloating over her unearned loot. That was Daniel's first and last attempt at seeking sexual gratification through the medium of professional providers.

There was no immediate or even remote chance of Daniel finding a solution to his problem. His very nature had excluded him from any other female company during his marriage and his lack of social ability had now left him in a thoroughly lonely situation. As he was now the indisputable owner of Highfield and therefore a man of some note in the neighbourhood, he did not doubt but that, once the situation was advertised as it were, there would be no shortage of women who would be happy to exchange their spinsterhood or merely their virginity for a position of power in what they would see as a wealthy household. But Daniel Robinson was not one to accept power sharing and most especially with a woman. With Jane it had been different; a perfectly complementary partnership which he could never envisage being repeated and it had had a basis in genuine love. No, he could not imagine that this sort of happy union could ever be possible again.

* * * * *

Daniel was in a remarkably cheerful frame of mind as he rode back from Malton late one afternoon. He had just attended the November hirings and had taken on two new horse lads to replace the two who were leaving. They were both young, healthy looking lads and, what is more, both had seemed very keen to work at Highfield. He thought he had detected in each a real love of horses and they reminded him of himself when he first was taken on by Richard Farlam. He had called in at the Green Man for a meal and had stayed chatting to one or two farming acquaintances for perhaps rather longer than he should but he had enjoyed the company and the straight talk as well as the friendly banter, which always took place on such occasions after the first pint or two had gone down. Perhaps remarkably, given the traumatic time he had lived through, Daniel was still a very moderate partaker of alcohol, imbibing only occasionally and always to a moderate extent so that today he was still very much in control of his thoughts and actions but in that mellow condition which allowed him to look favourably on the world at large.

He recalled with pleasure the happy occasion of Naomi's wedding a few weeks ago. She certainly had looked happy and there had been a general atmosphere of goodwill and cheerfulness amongst all the guests. Not that there had been many. With Tom there you didn't need many. Always the centre of attention with his jokes and lively sense of fun, he seemed capable of always being able to say the right thing, teasing the young girls, flattering the older women and yet remaining a man's man. Daniel was envious of all his brother's abilities which contrasted with his own rather dour personality. But dour or not, it was impossible to remain dull and serious for long in Tom's company and he had enjoyed the day enormously. A surprise visit had been made by his Lordship, who had turned up with a handsome present for the couple, and although he didn't stay long he made himself pleasantly known to the principal guests. There had been a friendly nod and handshake for Daniel and an enquiry after the children. It seemed that his Lordship had put behind him any resentment at the rude reception he had received from Daniel at Richard Farlam's funeral and Daniel was content that this was so. In fact, if pressed, he would have had to acknowledge that his earlier antipathy had been entirely dissipated now that he found himself in similar circumstances – as a land owner with all the problems and responsibilities which that entailed. The class barrier would never be breached, he knew well enough, but at least there could be a mutual respect.

It had been a long day, setting off for Malton as he had done at 5:30 in the morning, whilst it was still dark, and arriving some five hours later. His business concluded and his convivial lunch despatched at the Green Man, he set off home again but it was dark long before he returned to Highfield, as he had known it would be. He had taken his time, not wanting to risk injury to himself or his horse. The children would be long abed by the time he returned but he would make it up to them tomorrow. Late though it was however, there were still lights burning at both the Hall and the old Farm when he rode into the yard and dismounted. He stabled the horse and then entered the Hall to be met by trembling and tearful Lizzie who fell to her knees and howled

"T'wern't my fault maister. T'wern't my fault really. They just slipped away when I wasn't looking. I wouldn't have ever wanted any harm come to the little lad an' I've always done my best for them both. It just wern't my fault; t'wer an accident."

The feeling of contentment vanished immediately of course and a mild panic overtook him. Seizing the girl and shaking her violently he shouted

"The children! What's happened? Where are they?"

Shaken about so roughly the girl could hardly speak but she pointed across to the farm and gasped out "Miss Buckram, she has 'em both."

Without ceremony, he dropped the girl on the floor and raced across to the old farm. There was a light burning and, again without ceremony, he burst through the door to find Ruth sitting alone in the front room. She was sewing but put down her work and rose to her feet immediately he came in. Desperate with anxiety he took her by the shoulders and in a shaking voice enquired

"Where are they, Ruth? What has happened to them. That stupid girl said something about an accident".

"They're both upstairs and asleep Mr Robinson" she replied calmly "there's nothing to worry about now."

"But the accident; has there been an accident; are they hurt?"

"Well, yes, Richard has been hurt but he'll be all right. Doctor has been to see him and he says so."

"What has he done Ruth, please tell me." cried Daniel, fearing the worst.

"He's lost two fingers, Mr Robinson. Not very nice I know but it could have been worse."

Daniel stared at her mutely for a moment and then with more control he enquired if he could go up to see them.

"Of course Mr Robinson. They're in the little room at the front but please don't wake them, they're nicely settled now."

Daniel nodded and, much more calmly now, he thanked Ruth and agreed not to disturb them. "I just want to see with my own eyes " he said apologetically. Ruth smiled and turned away to produce that panacea for all problems, a cup of tea.

The children were lying together in a bed which was barely large enough for the two of them. Daniel guessed that they had insisted on being together and Mary had fallen asleep with one arm draped across her brother's chest. He lay sleeping soundly with his left arm outside the covers, the heavy bandage on his hand showing signs of blood having soaked through. It was dry he noted and so the bleeding had presumably stopped. Peering anxiously at the little face, he saw that the cheeks were tear stained as indeed were those of his sister and the pillow showed evidence of much weeping. But they were asleep and they seemed comfortable. With nothing else to do, he went downstairs to find Ruth pouring the tea. She persuaded him to sit and take the cup whilst she prepared to tell the story as she knew it.

It seemed that the children had been out on their own playing and had got into the barn, where all sorts of machinery and implements were stored. They had played there for some time and eventually had inspected the turnip chopping machine. Mary was strong enough to turn the handle and set the blades whirring inside which had entertained them for a while but then Richard had asked if she could give him a ride, by continuing to turn, whilst he stood on the cranked axis of the handle. Willing to try, she had helped her brother to climb up and then set to with a will to turn the handle over. She succeeded rather too well and, overbalancing, the little lad had reached out to grab some support, his hand going inside the machine. The keen blades had done the rest, slicing off the first and second fingers of his left hand. Everyone in the area had heard the screams and the source was soon tracked down. Lizzie had not responded and was nowhere in evidence so Ruth had taken charge and taken both children into the farmhouse. There she had held the maimed hand under the running tap and then bound it tightly with strips cut from one of her clean shifts. Both children were given drinks of sweet tea to try to settle them and avert shock, whilst a lad had been sent to find Doctor McClaren. The doctor had arrived an hour or so later and, having taken off the bandages and inspected the damage, had anointed the wounds with some coloured liquid before asking Ruth to bandage the hand up again.

"He seemed quite pleased with what ah'd done" she said modestly. "He asked where you were and said he'd come by later tonight to talk to you" she concluded and there was a brief pause as Daniel digested all this information.

Now that there was clearly no life threatening problem Daniel was in a much clearer and calmer state of mind. He thanked Ruth for her prompt attention to the situation and enquired why she had put them to bed in the old farm house. Why not their own bedroom? Uncharacteristically, Ruth answered rather hesitantly.

"I didn't think t'were quite fit Mr Robinson" she said with her face averted.

Daniel stared at her silently for a second or two and then enquired "And where was Lizzie during all this; didn't she come across to help?" Ruth seemed to be even more uncomfortable at this question. " She was asleep Mr Robinson, we 'ad a right job on, waking 'er up and making 'er understand what 'ad happened when we did find 'er." Daniel regarded her steadily for a moment more and then said quietly "Thank you Ruth, I'll be over to see them first thing but call me at once if there is any trouble with Richard."

He turned and left abruptly, striding purposefully towards the Hall intending to find Lizzie and the expression on his face boded ill for the girl. His anxiety had been replaced with an anger which increased with every step he took She had disappeared and was doubtless hiding in her bedroom but before seeking her out Daniel looked around him at the kitchen. It was really in a very dreadful condition when one gave it even the most casual inspection. Even in the poor light of the oil lamp the evidence of neglect was blatantly obvious. He pondered over this, realising that it must have been so this morning too, and the morning before, and so on backwards in time. It had been there for him to see but he had not done so. His preoccupation with his own problems and feelings had blinded him to everything beyond his immediate environment in the more formal part of the house which he had been recently using. The scullery was worse. Pots piled up in the sink, remnants of meals on plates set down haphazardly on work tops and a general clutter and disorder signified total carelessness on the part of the servant in charge. He proceeded up to the children's bedroom and what he saw there was little better. He could well understand Ruth's reluctance to leave the children in these filthy and uncared for surroundings and he burnt with shame at what she had seen there. His anger had reached boiling point now but it was directed principally against himself. How could he have been so self centred as to be unaware of a situation which had clearly existed for some time? How could he have neglected the welfare of his little children, seeking to avoid the burden of responsibility by thrusting it on the shoulders of one who was manifestly unfit to assume it? And how could he have broken so shamefully the promise he had made so glibly to his dying wife? No, blameworthy Lizzie might be, but it was he who was the most guilty. He should have perceived her unsuitability, made more strenuous efforts to find more and better staff, and certainly he should have kept as good a look out on his home as he did on the farm. Well, she would have to go and he would ask Ruth to care for Mary and Richard whilst he found a replacement. And he would find one, whatever the cost in time or money. He was debating whether or not to pitch her out now or on the following morning when the noise of a buggy entering the yard saved the girl from a very precipitate departure.

It was Andrew McClaren and Daniel welcomed him eagerly into the house full of questions. Andrew promised him the answers but commented that it would be an act of Christian charity to provide a suitable beverage for a man who had made the long drive to Highfield twice in one day. Smiling in spite of himself, Daniel led the way into the study where he poured a generous measure of brandy for the doctor. Feeling the need himself for a good relaxant, Daniel poured a large scotch and they sat down for Andrew to begin his tale. It was essentially as Ruth had recounted it earlier. The fingers, said Andrew, had been neatly sliced off between the first and second joints. The blades had been sharp enough to avoid any tearing which would have made the situation far worse. Furthermore the machine, when he inspected it later, seemed to be relatively clean.

"That wee lassie Ruth did a grand job too" he said. "I could not have done a better bandaging myself and she had ensured the wound was clean before putting it on. Furthermore she had had the sense to apply a permanent pressure to stop the bleeding. To be honest I had little to do when I got here."

"Aye, and she insisted on bedding them down in the farm house too" Daniel put in.

"Well yes, now that is something I need to discuss with you Daniel" said Andrew McClaren somewhat awkwardly and he took a good pull on his brandy before continuing. He set down his glass with a slight expression of distaste and exclaimed " Nae laddie, nae, I thought you knew better than to drown a good cognac with water!"

"But I – – – – " Daniel stared at his guest with a sickening suspicion and then quickly took a sip of his hitherto untasted whisky. It was almost pure water with just enough spirit in to retain the colour. Putting a hand up to silence the doctor he rose and went to his cabinet from whence he extracted all the bottles of liquor which were present. There were not many, a sherry, a port and some Madeira. Taking a clean glass he poured a sample of each and drank it. All had been similarly doctored with liberal amounts of water.

"Aye, now I see" he said ruefully. "Something once made me do a check but I just looked at the levels. Never thought to try the contents! Well now we know why they had trouble waking the girl up. Why did it have to take an accident to my little lad to wake me up to what has been going on?"

"I don't think any of us knew about the drink Daniel but we could see the effects of the bad housekeeping and frankly I did try to warn you on a few occasions. You just didn't want to listen. But never mind that; what are you going to do now?"

Andrew regarded his young friend intently. Daniel remained silent for a while and then spoke his thoughts aloud.

"Aye, well she'll have to go and quickly too. She'll be off the place tomorrow morning sharp. I can't bring the children back to an empty house, and a dirty one at that. No, I'll ask Ruth if she'll keep them on for a while at the old farmhouse while I get myself sorted out. It's not just a good housekeeper I want though; I need a mother for them bairns, a wife for myself an' all. But where to start?" He looked across at the doctor and smiled grimly." I've not been one for mixing with other people very much and especially the womenfolk. I'm not good at it and I fear there's not many women who'd take to me either but I suppose I shall have to make a try. How do I go about it Andrew?"

The latter laughed in reply, "You should not be asking a confirmed old bachelor how to enter the marriage stakes my boy! What I can do however is try to re-establish you in polite society after which you will have to do you're own work. I cannot say that I can think of any 'ladies in waiting' however but if you persevere something will turn up. Your social rehabilitation comes first however!"

Daniel merely grunted in reply. Andrew refused another watered down cognac announcing his intention to depart and in truth Daniel was pleased to see him go. He had a lot of thinking to do.

On the following morning the lads in the old farm house were astonished to find themselves sharing the breakfast table with their employer. The news of the accident to little Richard was of course common knowledge and there were hesitant and awkward remarks of sympathy and queries as to the state of his health this day. Daniel, who had been upstairs to check for himself, thanked them for their concern and was able to say that the boy had slept well and, although feeling rather sore, was resting a little more before getting up. Mary was playing nurse and all the more conscientiously because of her involvement with the cause of the accident. It was a strange feeling to be sitting once again at this well remembered table in the company of all the horse lads and Daniel rather enjoyed the experience, despite the fact that the conversation did not flow as easily as it might have done had he not been there. But muted and circumspect as it was, this conversation was comforting and homely, whilst the hot breakfast was satisfying. With Ruth bustling about in the background and fussing over his meal it was impossible to prevent feelings of nostalgia from sweeping over him. When everyone had left the table to return to work, Daniel spoke briefly to Ruth, asking her if she would be good enough to keep the children at the farm house and look after them for a few days. He answered her unspoken question by telling her that Lizzie had departed. That had been his first task of the day and the unhappy girl had been dismissed with the exact amount of money owing to her. There had been no finishing bonus, nor any deduction of money for the consumption of his drink but she had withered under his scornful dressing down for her lapses and had crept quietly away as soon as was possible. She had not received, nor indeed had expected, a reference.

Ruth had professed herself as only too willing to look after the little ones and, when she heard that Daniel was to be away for the day, returning in the evening. she insisted he attend supper with them all. He was not loath to accept this invitation but with no other explanation of his plans he saddled up his horse and rode off towards Baytown. It was late afternoon when he returned, somewhat travel stained, and going straight to the Hall he disappeared inside to re-emerge some time later having washed and changed. He hailed one of the lads who was crossing the yard and asked him to call in at the farm house and ask Miss Buckram if she could spare him a few minutes to see him in his study. When Ruth appeared she had brought the children with her and Daniel greeted them with cheerful enthusiasm, praising his son for the manly way in which he bore his wound and consoling the guilt ridden Mary. Both of them brightened considerably when they opened the little packets of sweetmeats he had brought for them and Daniel ushered them into the kitchen to deal with these presents whilst, he said, he had business to discuss with Miss Buckram in the study. Totally mystified, Ruth took the chair he indicated whilst he sat opposite her behind his desk. She was not to remain in ignorance for long and, when she learnt the purpose of this interview, the ground opened at her feet.

Bluntly, and typically so, Daniel went straight to the point.

"I rode over to Cloughton this afternoon to see Walter Simpson. I have taken him on to be my foreman and Mrs Simpson will take over the job of hind. They will be starting in a month's time and so I will be needing you and George to move out by then. It's not that you have been unsatisfactory in your job Ruth" he said, looking steadily at her stricken face, " It's just a matter of efficiency and economy; I'm sure you can see that."

Ruth could indeed see it, all too clearly. But she could see also a frightening prospect for the future. She knew that in many ways she had been extraordinarily fortunate in retaining a position for so long, where she had a roof over her head and subsistence not only for herself but also for her father, where she could care for him properly, protect him, keep him out of trouble and see that his days were spent happily. She was sure that she could find another position where she could live in, was sure that Mr Robinson would provide her with a good reference but where would she find a place which would accept George as well? That, she knew, she could never do and her mind cast about desperately examining the alternatives. They were few and all unpleasant. Her father needed fairly constant care and she had no one who could provide that for her. Her aunt and uncle could not cope with him in their little cottage on The Bolts for anything other than the briefest possible time and she would certainly not consider asking her married cousins with their families; they would refuse and be hurt and embarrassed at having to do so. It would have to be a residential institution but the only one relatively nearby, which she could envisage would take him, was the asylum at Scarborough. The thought of him lost and friendless in that uncaring establishment was more than she could bear. Raising her eyes to look directly into those of Daniel she whispered

"But my father, Mr Robinson, my poor old father, what will become of him?"

"Aye, t'will be difficult I dare say" was the reply. "Your relatives can't help I suppose?"

They could not help, nor could anyone else and with this realisation Ruth broke down and wept. She cried soundlessly but with shoulders shaking until words came from across the table which jolted her back under control.

"Aye, well I can see that you have a real problem but there is maybe one way you can get over it."

With faint hope rising in her heart she raised her head again to look once more into that direct gaze opposite. It was fortunate that her constitution was sufficiently robust to sustain the second bombshell to be delivered in the span of two minutes.

"If you were to agree to marry me Ruth, you and George could both move into the Hall. You would be very well provided for and George would have a secure home as long as you remained here with me." He continued over the astonished, nay dumbfounded, silence. " You see Ruth I am in need of a mother for my children. I do confess that I have failed badly in the promise I made to my late wife. I have not given them the care and the protection which I ought to have done. Oh I know I can say that I have had my work to do and I did have a lass to look after them but I also know that it is a poor excuse. I have let them down and must make amends and put things right as soon as may be."

Stunned into silence by his opening words, Ruth perceived a ray of light and hope which she quickly seized upon. "Well of course Mr Robinson; you need a good housekeeper and a nanny for the bairns and I'd be more than happy to take on such a job."

As she smiled hopefully at him Daniel shook his head. "No Ruth; that's not enough. I am wanting a wife. That would have to be part of the bargain."

A torrent of thoughts passed through her mind and she blanched as she realised the enormity of the choice she was being forced to make. In a moment of vivid self realisation Ruth saw that this was one major decision which she had to make herself. Confident in her ability to make the decisions necessary for the management of a household, the small day to day choices of action in the running of her own life, Ruth saw clearly that hitherto she had been protected from the need to make important decisions either by her parents or more latterly by the kind but firm advice of her aunt and uncle. Now she saw that in this matter she was on her own. To be married, yes! A goal for any young woman in this age and especially when that marriage was likely to bring a comfortable lifestyle with it. But to marry this man, so unbending, so direct and purposeful, so stern and hard – – –

so much older than her. And how could she abandon her sweetheart Jonathon? He of whom she had dreamed so often and so long. She loved him. And he loved her, didn't he? Even now she summoned up a vision of his face before her and recalled some of the happy times they had spent together. But even as she relived those moments she also recalled that conversation with her aunt and wondered again at the lack of progress in what she fondly imagined was his wooing of her. Perhaps it would never be that she would become his wife. And in the meantime what of her father? Six years, yes that was about the difference between her and the man who had just proposed. Well perhaps six years was not so much after all. It could be made to work she thought. But she didn't love him! And he didn't love her. He wanted a mother for his children and a woman in his bed. A small tremor ran through her at that thought. The thought was interrupted by Daniel who addressed her again in what he hoped was a more gentle and persuasive manner.

"Ruth I cannot try to make out that I hold a great love for you. I know this is not a romantic affair; not the sort of thing that young lasses dream of I suppose." He searched through his mind for a phrase and came up with one of Jane's. "It would be a sort of working arrangement." His smile was gentle and persuasive. "But I can offer you kindness and care; a comfortable living although there will be plenty of work. I can offer you a permanent home for yourself and for George." He paused and then continued more awkwardly. "I should think you would know what a deep feeling there was between me and Jane. We didn't bother to hide it I suppose. I can't give you that feeling Ruth, not that sort of love; not yet anyway." he finished rather lamely.

It was this break in his certainty, this weakness in his determined manner, which clinched matters for Ruth. She looked at him again and saw a worried man, a vulnerable man, an earnest man trying his best to put his case but also trying to be completely honest.

"There is someone I must tell you about Mr Robinson." she announced.

"Oh aye, young Mr Stormson I suppose." was the reply.

"You knew I was walking out with him?" she asked in surprise.

"Ah did that. And from what Ah've heard you'll probably still be walkin' wi' 'im at doomsday."

The lapse into a broad dialect and the rather wicked grin were both designed to lighten the atmosphere and it had an effect. Ruth produced her first smile for some considerable time.

"I'll need to speak to my uncle and aunt." she said, knowing however that her decision had already been made.

"Aye, of course but I can tell you that they approve the match" he replied complacently.

Again Ruth was astonished. "How do you know that?" she enquired.

"First thing I did this morning. Went down to Baytown and asked their permission to wed you. Grand woman, your aunt. Saw things properly straight away."

Daniel had indeed visited the Jenson house that morning. Martha Jenson had been glancing out of the window when she saw a young boy pointing out her door to a man and then rush off with a shiny penny clutched in his hand. Doubtless it was destined to be transferred in short order to the till of Mrs Boddy, the confectioner. She had recognised her visitor immediately as Daniel Robinson of Highfield and wondered with some alarm what he might have come to tell her. Most of the news from Highfield had been bad in recent years. She opened the door to his knock and, after an exchange of civilities, invited him into the tiny parlour. Daniel's approach had been as blunt as he was to be later with Ruth but if anything more businesslike. Martha Jenson was nobody's fool, a pragmatist and a realist. She had quickly appreciated the incredible stroke of luck it was for her niece to be offered such a match. She had appreciated too the honesty of the man in his recounting of the circumstances which caused him to make this offer and his lack of pretence in the matter of professing an overwhelming love for the girl. She had nodded understandingly, when he had insisted that he wanted a wife and not just a housewife. Martha told him of the relationship between Ruth and Jonathon Stormson.

"He would have been a good catch too; maybe even better than yourself Mr Robinson!"

However, she laughed grimly and admitted that in her opinion Ruth would never make that catch. But even the pragmatic have their reservations.

"I just want your assurance Mr Robinson, as a gentleman, that you will always treat her well and with kindness."

Daniel had been able to look her straight in the eye and give that assurance. They parted on good terms those two, he to Cloughton to interview the Wilsons and she to begin formulating wedding arrangements. It is interesting to speculate as to whether Martha Jenson would have retained her good opinion of Daniel had she known of the terrible blackmail he was about to inflict upon her niece in terms of her fears for her father.

Now, up at Highfield Hall, Ruth made that fateful decision.

"I still think I should go and talk to my aunt and uncle" she said "but I can give you my answer now Mr Robinson. Thank you for asking me to marry you and the answer is yes."

Daniel beamed with pleasure, not unmixed with relief. "Well that's grand, just grand but there's one more thing."

Ruth thought she was inured against shock by now but she awaited the next words in trepidation nonetheless.

"It'll have to be Daniel now. Ruth and Daniel. It always used to be a few years ago and now 'twill need to be so again – for appearances sake of course."

Ruth smiled and said "Yes, Daniel. So it will be."

But why, after saying something nice like that, was it necessary to spoil it with an excuse for the familiarity?

The wedding was a small affair. Attended by all the family of course and a few chosen friends but not the occasion which Ruth had liked to dream about. Her uncle Jethro had given her away. George was present but had been kept discreetly in the background. Tom being away at sea, Daniel had asked Andrew McClaren to stand with him. Jessica had been a matron of honour and Mary had performed her duties as bridesmaid with great pride and seriousness. Little Richard had enjoyed all the fuss and displayed his mutilated hand to any who would care to look. But to the eyes of many the church looked disappointingly empty and there was somehow lacking the unrestrained joy and celebration which normally attended such functions. Ruth certainly noticed this but put on a brave face as she processed out through the porch on the arm of her husband. The weather seemed to conspire in this low key atmosphere. It was in fact quite dreary. There was no rain as such; just a very fine drizzle associated with the sea fret which obscured all but the nearest features of the locality. It was a wedding which seemed to want to become submerged in obscurity and anonymity.

As the party proceeded down the path across the churchyard, they passed within a few yards of a newly erected headstone. There having been a year for the ground to settle, it had been deemed safe now to place the memorial stone in position. The fresh white stone was one of the few relatively bright features of the scene. The fine drizzle had thoroughly covered it however and droplets of water were coursing down the chiselled lines of writing, to flow over the smooth lower cheeks of the stone. The mason had admired those words, as he laboured to reproduce them with his skilled hands. They read:

Here Lies interred a chaste and virtuous wife,
Who smiled at death and calm resigned her life.
Her soul, dismantled of this cumbrous clay,
To bliss eternal now has winged its way.
Long live the offspring, grant them Power Divine,
That all the mother in the children shine.

CHAPTER 8

THE SHIPWRECK

Daniel was seated in his study, where he ruminated over a newspaper report predicting hard times for the farming community because of 'indiscriminate replacement of the honest labourer with modern machinery'. He had read the article with some contempt, coming to the conclusion that the 'expert' had no real comprehension of what it was possible to achieve by adaptation of the labour force and what the real problems were for farmers. Over the years he had made several changes in the way Highfield was run, all in the name of progress or improvement, and he regretted none of them. He had always admired the way in which Richard Farlam had stayed up to the mark in terms of modern equipment and the institution of modern farming practice, so much so, that he had determined to do likewise. Over the years since Farlam's death there had been quite a few changes. New machinery was of course a part of this and Daniel was pleased with his acquisitions. The mechanical reaper, which had been developed in America, was an absolute boon and could cut fifteen acres in a matter of ten hours or so – a tremendous saving in man hours – which had enabled him to lay off some of his work force but, whilst it had improved the profit margins on the estate, it had certainly not gone down too well with the populace of the village and surrounding area.

There had been some dark mutterings. Well they would have to live with the changing times, as he did himself. There was another device he had heard of as being developed in America but had not yet reached these shores. This was an automatic binding machine, which apparently picked up the corn and spat out bound sheaves at the rear. Another potential saving in man power, which would doubtless alienate him further from the labouring fraternity but he would certainly look at it when it became available.

At least he was employing men in the reclamation of the land he had recently purchased, adjacent to and just to the north of the estate. This had been a stretch of the moor owned by his Lordship, who had been hoping to sell it to the company proposing to build a railway line from Scarborough to Whitby. In the expectation that this would come about, his Lordship had overspent rather unwisely on other things so that, when the railway project fell through, he was in slight financial difficulties. Although these were likely to be only temporary, he had been compelled to offer the land for sale but the local farming community had been unenthusiastic in the main. There was only Daniel who had been interested but he kept this interest under his hat until he was sure that he was the only prospective purchaser, at which time he made a casual approach to the castle land agent. With a show of great reluctance and hesitation he allowed himself to make a much reduced offer for the land, angrily dismissed at first but eventually accepted after a small upward adjustment. The point was that, although the land was uncultivated heather and bracken, which would need great expense and effort to intake into a useful agricultural element of the Highfield estate, Daniel was convinced that the railway scheme would be resurrected at some time in the future and his investment would be worth considerably more. Meanwhile he was trying to accomplish an improvement in its condition by the eradication of the heather and the spreading of liberal amounts of lime to lessen the acidity of the soil.

This had been another lesson he had learnt from Richard Farlam, who had realised very early in his farming career the advantages of caring for the soil by the addition of minerals and fertilisers. Many years ago he had arranged a standing contract with the gasworks to deliver ammonia liquor for spreading on his fields and recently Daniel had gone one step further by purchasing one of Mr Chandlers new drills, which automatically poured the liquor into the holes where the seeds were deposited There had been much shaking of heads in the farming community as they talked of the expense involved in this practice. The cost of ammonia sulphate at two shillings and sixpence for nine hundred gallons and then the task of diluting this with five times its volume of water made many cast doubts on the sanity of Mr Farlam but, as the years went by and details of the yields from his land became known, there was a revision of opinion and most farmers now adopted the habit of adding some form of fertiliser to their fields, spending hard earned money on the purchase of guano for example with a consequent improvement in their own crops. Although he bought in some additives, Daniel still thought that natural fertiliser was best and he realised how fortunate Highfield was in its possession of a large herd of big horses. Huge middens were produced from the waste products of these animals and this was all led out to be spread over the land, as had happened from time immemorial.

So then he could congratulate himself upon the healthy finances of the estate but what of his private life? He felt that here too he had made a satisfactory arrangement. Ruth had settled down well in her role as housekeeper, surrogate mother and sexual partner. He had no complaints as to her compliance with the conditions he had set down when their bargain was struck; she provided all the services he required without fuss and with great success. She had won over the love and respect of his children even to the extent that they called her 'mother' and thought of her as such. Mary had only a slight remembrance of her real mother, whilst Richard had none. Now, eight years after their marriage, there were three more little ones, Martha, Thomas and Rebecca, and all five children regarded themselves as part of the same family, all subject to the same treatment and with the same privileges.

Daniel could not rid himself of the recollection that Ruth had loved, probably still loved, another. Although it might be thought faintly ridiculous to suppose it, he was secretly terrified that the handsome young Stormson boy, resplendent in his captains uniform, might reappear on the scene, might persuade Ruth to elope with him and leave Daniel to be once again the sole carer for his children – now augmented to five! It was the welfare of these children that most bothered him; on his own he would be able to cope well enough, he told himself. As always happened when he fell to these thoughts, he reasoned that she would never abandon her own children and Jonathon would not be prepared to take on a ready made family of three – would he? His name was never mentioned in the house; Ruth made no reference to him in any way nor had ever done so since their wedding day. However she had met him. Daniel knew that, thanks to the prying eyes and wagging tongues of Baytown. Innocent enough perhaps, but they had met and talked on at least one occasion. Oh well he could do nothing more than make her living conditions so good as to minimise the risk of her leaving. The death last year of old George had removed the hold he had over her but she had seemed content to stay on, which had been a relief.

He had been subconsciously aware of the strong winds blowing outside but a sudden sharp blast rattled the windows violently and he came back to the present abruptly. It was time for his supper; he was hungry. Where was the lass? Ruth was in the kitchen preparing the evening meal, which he was so looking forward to. It was to be a beef stew, which she knew was a favourite and which was certainly appropriate, given the dreadful weather conditions prevailing at that time.

The year 1880 had been very poor and was being followed by a new year which seemed determined to be even worse. During early January the entire country had been blanketed by snow, which showed no signs of melting. Indeed successive wintry showers had increased the depth of the snow and paralysed communications. It was impossible to work the land and the continuing high winds made it necessary to keep a good watch out for damage to buildings and especially their roofs.

Ruth knew the enforced idleness was frustrating for Daniel but at least it gave him more time to be with the children. She smiled as she remembered the scene in the nursery earlier that evening as Daniel lay on the bed surrounded by the packed bodies of the four older children, whilst he read to them from their favourite story book. Little Thomas could not really understand more than a fraction of what was being read, whilst Mary considered herself to be far too old for these babyish tales but nonetheless they all hung upon every word of the history, as it was interpreted by their father. Daniel read with great solemnity and a certain amount of drama, which had perhaps not been intended by the author, so that from time to time one or more of them would clutch at his arm in terror. Ruth could clearly see that he enjoyed these bedtime sessions enormously and she was gratified to note that there was no difference in his attitude to her children as opposed to Jane's. She envied him his ability to read to them so well; her own command of the three R's was comparatively poor and she was glad to leave the chore to Daniel, who, she knew, was quite proud of the progress he had made in this direction.

She had no regrets for the bargain she had struck eight years ago. It had been as he had said. There was plenty of work for her to do, most especially in the care of the family but also in the management of the house. However Daniel had seen to it that she had every comfort and had engaged Janet, a young girl from Hawsker, to help in the house. Ruth had felt awkward and embarrassed about this at first but, as the young lass clearly saw nothing untoward in an arrangement where Ruth gave the instructions and she carried them out, then Ruth too had slowly accepted the situation and now actually enjoyed the ability to share the workload and most especially in the least attractive tasks. It was quite good fun having a servant! Ruth smiled and paused for a moment to reflect upon the magical transformation of her circumstances.

There was of course one missing ingredient. She knew it was silly but she couldn't help thinking how nice it would have been if she had been able to marry for love. She remembered the dreams she had nourished of marital bliss with Jonathon. He was now a fully qualified master mariner and, as far as she knew, still unmarried. There had been one awkward meeting three years ago, when they had almost collided in the main street of Baytown, she on her way to the Jensen house, and he hurrying up to above town. He had risen to the occasion, congratulating her on her marriage and enquiring after her family. He was full of news about his own career but she had been disappointed to feel that he was not at all upset about the way things had turned out; no recriminations for having married without telling him, no expression of regret for what might have been. He was as attractive as ever, charming and cheerful. Far too cheerful she thought.

Ruth left the completion and serving of the meal to Janet and went to call her husband through to the dining room. She had got used to the idea now of eating in this separate room rather than the big kitchen, although it had seemed an unnecessary procedure at first to transport all the food from its place of origin to the opposite end of the house. Amazing what a difference a maid makes however in this respect she thought with a smile and she did recognise that it was necessary to draw a line between themselves and young Janet. Here it was in the dining room then that they usually ate now and, most especially of course, on those rare occasions when they entertained company. Ruth was glad that they were rare, as she had not yet been able to feel entirely happy with visitors in the house. The exception was Andrew McClaren, who had made her feel from the start that it really was her own home. Andrew was getting on in years now and did not make the journey over to Highfield so often. He certainly would not be turning out again until the weather moderated and Ruth made a mental note to pay him a visit and take over some fresh baking. She really liked Andrew and the feeling was mutual. He was adept at making her feel she was an equal in their company, often consulting her about cooking and household management and making her laugh at some of the bizarre mistakes he had made, as an ageing bachelor who had recently lost his housekeeper. At first he had been as astonished as the rest of the local populace, when Daniel had married Ruth but he had quickly appreciated the wisdom of the choice and approved heartily, which had pleased Daniel immensely in view of the respect he had for his old friend's opinion.

The meal was eaten in silence but it was a companionable one and Ruth enjoyed watching her husband partaking of his food with such evident relish. There was a sigh of satisfaction as he pushed his empty plate back but Ruth could not resist the temptation to prod him a little by enquiring if he had enjoyed the dinner. "Aye, t'were passing fair" was the response and she knew she would have to be content with this apparently faint praise. She looked carefully for signs of humour but could detect none. Nevertheless she suspected that Daniel was playing a little game when he responded to her enquiries in this way, as he so often did. Or maybe she was wrong. Perhaps he thought that the very fact that he had eaten the food should have been praise enough! But tonight was surprisingly different for he amplified his reply "Just the right meal for a night like this" and his words were underlined by a timely loud rattling of the windows as the wind struck again. He grimaced at the sound and continued, "Ah'll need to go out and see all's well. But ah'll not be over long and maybe we can 'ave an early night."

"Very good Daniel. I'll help Janet clear away but you'll likely need a hot drink when you come back in."

He nodded his assent and went off to light the lantern and struggle into his heavy coat before leaving the warm house for the freezing conditions outside. The brief opening of the outside door admitted the wind, which had been trying unsuccessfully to enter all evening, and it set the curtains flapping and caused something to rattle noisily in the kitchen.

Ruth was glad that she didn't have to venture out and could enjoy the comfort of the warm rooms and anticipate a warm bed. She had understood Daniel's remark about an early night perfectly. After eight years she knew him well enough to appreciate that he would want sex tonight. Well that was all right. She recalled the dread with which she had first anticipated the act on their wedding night and the surprise she had felt at being so gently treated. Although she had no yardstick to go by, she thought Daniel was quite a demanding man as far as his sexual needs were concerned but, while she was frequently called upon to satisfy them, she had never felt abused or roughly treated. He could be very considerate and seemed anxious to make it a pleasurable event for her. And he often succeeded she thought, feeling a little twinge of pleasant anticipation at the prospect of the union to follow. It was perhaps the Jensen blood in her veins which had allowed her to accept the inevitable and make the best of it, even to the point of enjoyment. So much for the notion that sexual relations could only be pleasurable if you were desperately in love with your partner. That had certainly been the received wisdom amongst her contemporaries when she was a young girl but she knew better now!

When Daniel stepped out of the house and crossed the yard, the wind fought him every inch of the way. He had to lean into it and use all of his considerable strength to make progress. Sporadically there were bursts of snow driven before the gale but it was not the quantity of the precipitation which caused the main problem; it was the gale itself. The wind was moving vast quantities of snow which had already fallen and piling it into the most fantastically shaped drifts. Paths were blocked, doorways filled, with the snow line often coming straight down from the roof in an unbroken sweep, totally obliterating any evidence of door or window beneath. As he approached the stables, the wind veered violently to the south and he stumbled under the sudden shift of pressure, nearly dropping the lantern. He lurched into the shelter of the stable block and found there Walter Simpson, who had preceded him in the task of checking on the horses. "Nasty night Walter" Daniel volunteered.

"Aye it is that and t'will be worse afore morning." was the cheerful reply.

The two men inspected the horses and agreed on a programme to share the chore of walking round all the buildings, stacks etc. This was precisely the sort of weather which could find the weaknesses in old walls and roofs, ripping tiles off and destroying a badly tied down haystack in minutes. They would not meet again unless a problem was located so wished each other a good night. Walter's parting words were "God help sailors on a night like this!" and Daniel nodded, his thoughts flying to his brother Tom, wondering where he might be and hoping he was safe.

* * * * *

There was no need for Daniel's concern over the safety of his brother. Hazards there may have been in the dockside public house in Portsmouth, but they were not of a maritime nature. As it was Tom was carousing merrily at a party to celebrate a mess-mates birthday. The ale was flowing, and, largely because of that, the girls all looked beautiful. There was laughter and song and warmth enough for men to forget the freezing conditions which would await them when they finally returned to their ship. In their happy state they gave no heed to the problems of others at sea. But there was at least one ship which was in peril that night and it was off the North Yorkshire coast struggling to make its way from Newcastle to London. The 'Visiter' was a Whitby registered collier brig of some 180 tons and was fully laden with coal. She had sailed from the Tyne two days earlier and had thrashed her way through violent seas down the coast reaching the vicinity of Flamborough Head by Tuesday afternoon. It had been dark as they passed Whitby and the driving snow had masked any lights which might have been visible as they came level with Baytown; the Master had looked in vain for signs of his hometown but had little time to spare for regrets.

She was an old vessel the 'Visiter', 57 years old in fact, and had given valuable and reliable service over that time plying between Wear, Tees or Tyne and the ports of London or Rochester. The ship was owned, as was quite common in those days, by a consortium of share holders all of whom lived in Baytown. The youngest of the 'Visiter's' shareholders, and its proud Master at this time, was Jonathon Stormson. Jonathon had been Master for the last two passages of this ship and he was proud of his responsibility. He was proud too of this sturdy, if ageing, ship; proud of her ability to weather the extraordinary sea conditions and the raging winds; proud of his crew, two of whom, including William Bell the Mate, were also from Baytown. The three teenagers who made up the rest of the six man crew were from London. But proud of his vessel as he was, the Master was not a little anxious about her condition. Bell had reported that she had been making water and the bilge pumps were in constant use to cope with the problem. Clearly the seams of the timbers were working under the violent motion of the waves and there was a need of some respite from the buffeting to ease the situation. It was late on the Tuesday afternoon, with the light fading, and they were approaching Flamborough Head. Perhaps, if he edged her inshore a little after they had passed the Flamborough light, he might benefit from the lee of that mighty headland. It was almost precisely at the moment when he might have executed this manoeuvre that fate, through the medium of the weather, struck a mighty and fatal blow to the unlucky vessel. The wind had eased just a trifle giving cause for some relief on the part of all on board, when suddenly it burst upon them again in renewed energy and from the totally unexpected direction of the South East. The ship was taken aback and it is a testament to the skill of captain and crew that she did not founder in that instant. By dint of superb handling, Jonathon was able to turn the ship so that she was running before the wind, now blowing at the level of a full gale. The noise was deafening with the wind shrieking in the rigging and the seas battering the hull. Remorselessly the 'Visiter' was being driven northwards and as the day wore on she began to lose much of her sail area as canvas was torn and blown away. The pattern of the swells set up by the earlier, persistent northerly winds was now being disrupted by the waves created by the South Easterly storm and this imparted an even more violent and unpredictable motion to the ship. The pounding which her timbers were sustaining was manifested by the gains which the water was now making in the bilge. The pumps were simply not coping. There was one small comfort to be taken from the disorderly wave pattern. Had there been a large following sea with huge swells, there would have been a danger of the ship being 'pooped'. The sails were now mostly blown away and her speed through the water would have likely been slower than that of the following waves, which could then have swept over the stern and swamped her. But even without that particular danger, in these prevailing conditions Jonathon knew that he was still in serious trouble. He needed shelter badly and for that he needed to know exactly where he was. Visibility was very bad and he was despairing of any hope of sighting land when a stroke of good fortune, the only one they had had so far, revealed a flashing light far away on the port bow. It was a familiar light with a familiar period of flashes. The 'Visiter' was level with Scarborough. There was no hope of reaching that haven, which in any case would provide no shelter from the southeaster which was driving them, so Jonathon resolved upon the only plan he could think of to save his ship and crew. He would take the vessel into Robin Hood's Bay. At 2:00 a.m. the 'Visiter' rounded the South Cheek and came to anchor, where hopefully she could ride out the storm.

It was not to be. Despite the continued efforts at the pumps by the exhausted men, the water was steadily gaining and Jonathon suspected the worst. By 6:00 a.m. it was clear that the vessel could not be saved and plans were laid for abandoning ship. The ship's longboat was launched and, with the time which they were granted by strenuous efforts at the pumps, they prepared her by stowing as much as they could find in the way of dry clothes, food and especially water. They were well aware that rescue could take a very long time in these dreadful conditions and tried to provision the boat with all they could think of which might be of value. A kedge anchor was laid to secure her position and she was tied to the 'Visiter' by two lines. The idea was that even when the brig finally sank the longboat would ride in the lee of the wreck and gain some shelter from the waves.

By 8:00 a.m. the water in the hold had reached a depth of five feet. Much lower in the water now, the ship's deck was being swamped by the waves. It was time to go. The Mate first entered the boat and oversaw the embarkation of the crew placing them carefully to preserve the trim of the little vessel. There remained on deck Jonathon and the youngest apprentice, Algie Dodd. The Master, clutching his papers and log book, shouted to the lad "I'll be last off," but Algie misheard the order in the general clamour of the storm and cast off the longboat. There was a shout of alarm from the boat as she drifted away but fortunately the kedge held the ground and she came to rest close enough to the brig to be sheltered from the full force of the waves.

"Can you swim Algie?" enquired Jonathon and the terrified boy, looking at the raging seas, nodded and said bravely

"A bit sir. But – – "

"Yes, I know Algie. We shall have to arrange for some help for you. We have the time."

Scouting around, Jonathon found some line and lashed the young apprentice to a life-buoy. When he was satisfied that it was secure he leant calmly against the rail with an arm on the boy's shoulder and waited.

"There's no rush to get wet Algie." he smiled down at the lad "but we'll go off together when needs must."

In fact it was nearly an hour later that the 'Visiter' finally sank at her anchor and the two remaining occupants jumped into the sea and swam to the boat, where they were hauled aboard by the rest of the crew. It was not yet daylight and, with the snow still flying in the fierce wind, it was a miserable task to peel off the saturated clothes and tug on the fresh dry ones which providentially they had stowed aboard earlier. Now it was a question of trying to keep warm as they waited for daylight and the chance of being spotted and rescued. Whilst he cheered his men up with the promise that this was only a matter of time, in his mind's eye Jonathon could see the useless hulk of the old Baytown lifeboat and he knew that help would have to come from further afield.

Three young beachcombers, sons of local fishermen, made the discovery which alerted the town to the plight of the mariners. At first light and on the falling tide they had ventured out along the shoreline looking for useful flotsam hurled up onto the beach by the tremendous waves. They discovered a huge piece of timber, which was in fact the quarterboard of the sunken brig and bore her name. It was a name of course which was very familiar to them and they ran back to the landing with their news. The coastguards soon spotted the remnants of the ship and, in her lee, the longboat which, their telescopes revealed, had people on board. It was nearly a mile out to sea, too far to be reached by rockets and so it would be necessary to effect a rescue by boat. The local fishermen however would not consider putting out to sea in the old Baytown lifeboat and indeed, when it was inspected by the coastguards, they absolutely forbade its use. There were several groups of people on the shore now and amongst them much discussion as to what could be done, the consensus being that the Whitby lifeboat should be sent for. It was the vicar, the Reverend Cooper, who sent telegrams from the King Street Post Office to both Whitby and Scarborough but the reply from the latter was disappointing. Commander Grant explained that he was unable to help as his tugs were aground in the harbour. He would send one and a lifeboat however as soon as conditions allowed.

In Whitby the message was received by the Harbour Master, Captain Gibson, shortly after 10:00 a.m. He was also the Lifeboat Secretary and reluctantly he called out Henry Freeman, the first cox. His reluctance was due to the fact that the Whitby boat had already been called out five times that night, a night that would be long remembered for the appalling conditions in which the crew had had to operate. The problem now was that the weather was, if anything, even worse this morning. Seldom on this coast does a wind stay in the south east quarter and true to form it had veered back round to the north east. Huge seas were breaking across the harbour mouth and it was quite impossible to take a boat out through the entrance. Even a tug could not survive the turmoil of the vicious seas, which would have hurled her against the piers and smashed her up. A brave man, as had been testified by his efforts already during the last twelve hours, Henry Freeman was adamant that it would be suicidal to attempt to sail from the harbour. Captain Gibson knew that he was right but, as he stared at the cox in despair, the latter spoke again.

"We'll just 'ave te tak 'er ower't top, Capn'."

The secretary gazed at him in disbelief.

"You mean haul her overland. Henry?" he exclaimed.

"Aye, that's reet. We could launch from the beach at Baytown reet enough. North Cheek would gi'e us plenty of shelter."

Captain Gibson stared at him for only a moment longer and then sprang into action.

"Right Henry, call out the lads and I'll see to the work force." But first of all he went to the Post Office and sent his reply. "Leaving with lifeboat at once. Send men and horses to meet us."

* * * * *

It was mid morning and, strangely, Daniel was sitting in the kitchen sharing a pot of tea with his wife. Despite his exertions during the previous night, Daniel had risen as early as usual but, having inspected the horses and consulted with Walter Simpson, he had agreed that there was nothing to be done except set on the lads to dig away the snow. Drifts which had been cleared the day before had re-formed, a dense blanket of white covered the entire landscape and there was obviously more to come but clearance had to be carried out again, just to enable people to get about from one building to another. Meanwhile Daniel sat chafing under his enforced idleness, whilst Ruth endured his irritability in silence punctuated by only the occasional sympathetic remark. She had just risen to replenish the pot of tea when a horse clattered into the yard, the sound of its hooves muffled somewhat by the snow. This was followed by a hammering on the door and, when

Ruth went to open it, a snow plastered figure stood on the threshold. With difficulty she recognised Robert Cooper, son of the vicar of Baytown, and she bade him enter quickly from the storm which still raged outside.

"Now then Bob, what brings you out on a day like this?" enquired Daniel, glad to have something to distract him.

"It's you I've come to see Mr Robinson. Father asks if you would come to help. There's been a shipwreck."

"Well now Ah'm not sure how I can be of help; I know little about the sea and less about ships." said Daniel somewhat mystified.

"No sir, it's your horses we need. You see they are trying to haul the Whitby boat overland to Baytown. It cannot be launched from the harbour because of the big seas that are running. We know there are survivors to be rescued and we know that some of them are men from our town."

"Oh aye" said Daniel "Then you'll know what ship it is?"

"Yes, she's the 'Visiter'. "

There was an audible gasp and the men turned to see Ruth holding a hand to her mouth, her face pale with shock. Daniel looked at her and enquired quietly

"His ship?"

Ruth nodded mutely. Daniel stood for a second or two regarding her steadily then turned abruptly to the messenger and said:

"Right then. I'll get three teams ready and bring them on as soon as possible. The lads will bring over another three an hour later to act as relief. Have they set off from Whitby yet?"

"They were just doing so as I left to come here but Heaven knows how far they will have managed to get. There are teams of men digging through the drifts from each end but the snow is terribly deep in some places."

Robert was relieved that his plea had not fallen on deaf ears. Daniel Robinson was known to be a difficult man at times but now he seemed to be charged with energy and willingness to help.

"I'll come with you to meet them" he said "Father says it would be as well for both groups to keep in touch and I am to be the go-between."

Daniel was busy donning his heavy outdoor garments but turned to Ruth before he left saying

"You'll want to be there when the lifeboat brings them all off. Don't try to go on your own; get one of the lads to ride with you as far as your Aunt's house."

With that he ushered the young Mr Cooper out of the door and set about organising the caravan of horses and equipment which would be needed to bring over the lifeboat. The teams made their way slowly across the icy wastes to the Whitby road and turned into it, pulling one small cart which contained traces, chains, spare collars, shovels and any other equipment which might be of use. The going was difficult and, despite the vast strength of the horses, they had to be assisted at times by the team of lads digging through the drifts. The main road was no better with huge sprawling drifts up to seven feet deep filling the track completely. The wind had sculpted them into fantastic shapes and on a less desperate occasion they would have been the cause for wonder and admiration, but as it was they were merely cursed, as aching limbs wielded shovel after shovel of the impediment out of the way. They encountered a group of travellers who had abandoned their horses and traps in the snow claiming that the road was impassable but Daniel studiously ignored them and pressed on. It was time consuming but eventually they reached Stainsacre and Daniel was disappointed to find no sign of the oncoming boat. He decided to ride on alone and soon encountered a huge gang of about seventy men all digging through the snow towards Baytown. They indicated that the lifeboat was immediately behind them, having just climbed the hill out of the town, and so he rode on to meet it. It was a sorry sight when he did so.

The 'Robert Whitworth' had been hauled by man power along the harbour side and over the bridge into Church Street. Here some horses had been harnessed to the carriage and a crowd of enthusiastic helpers had joined in the worthy endeavour. Men, women and children had seized shovels, willingly loaned by traders, and the cavalcade went off up the side of the river at a splendid rate. As soon as the gradient had increased however things slowed dramatically. The road was covered with ice lying beneath the snow and the carriage skidded wildly, the horses slipped on the treacherous surface and progress came to a halt. Once more the crowd assisted by fetching quantities of salt and sand. Even then it required the help of twenty men hauling on ropes in addition to the horses to persuade the carriage to move up the hill. Stops were frequent, the wheels being chocked to prevent any backward slide, but they persevered and were breasting the last rise out of the town when Daniel appeared. He was shocked when he saw the state of the horses. They were clearly exhausted and the sweat had frozen on their coats, whilst ice had stuck together all the hairs of their manes and tails. He met with Henry Freeman and the second cox, John Storr, who with all the rest of the boat's crew had been hauling on the ropes.

"Thank God you've come Robinson!" said John Storr "Would you take charge of the hauling now?"

Daniel was gratified by the confidence thus placed in him but knew that he was probably the best man for the job and assumed command immediately. He advised them to rest and unhitch the exhausted animals, sending them back to their stables. His own teams were coming up shortly, he claimed, and would be able to take over the job. And so it proved. The huge and powerful Clydesdales, comparatively fresh despite their journey from Highfield, moved the boat forward at an encouragingly rapid pace, following the path cleared by the advance party of diggers. Always appreciative of the worth of his wonderful animals, Daniel felt an immense pride as he watched them throw themselves into the harness and exert all their strength, continuing without shirking despite the terrible weather. Soon they overtook the men with the shovels and now progress slowed again. The second troop of horses arrived from Highfield and Daniel lost no time in replacing the tiring animals with the three new teams. Fresh and strong as they were, it was desperately hard work. It would have been worse were it not for the knowledge of the land which Daniel possessed and made good use of. He was able to lead the party over the easiest ground and at one time ordered a gate to be removed and the space widened, so that the boat could leave the road and take a short cut over an easier field path. There was a cheer as they linked up with the men who had been digging their way towards them from Robin Hood's Bay. Within a relatively short time they were standing at the top of Bay Bank. The journey from the harbour side, some five miles in distance and climbing six hundred feet, had taken three hours.

There now began the most difficult and dangerous part of the entire journey – the descent of the long bank through the village to the sea. Once again the ice was a potential hazard but, warned by Robert Cooper of the difficulties encountered in Whitby, the townsfolk had been generous in their help with the sanding of the streets. Daniel made the difficult decision of dispensing with the use of his horses on this stretch of the journey and sent them all back to their stables. He wanted to have a more sensitive control over the operation and a more rapid response to any untoward or precipitous movement. Ten men, mostly from the Whitby crew, were detailed to be in charge of the lifeboat itself and went between the shafts of the carriage. Meanwhile, a host of volunteers took up ropes attached to the body of the carriage and they set off again down through the village. Progress was necessarily slow and cautious, the road being very steep and the streets narrow. Passing the Laurel Inn was the tightest squeeze of all. John Storr told Daniel that there had been an inch to an inch and a half to spare as the lifeboat passed round the acute bend in the road by this public house. Daniel had laughed loudly at this intelligence and Storr had looked at him strangely. He was not to know that Daniel, greatly on edge by the tension of the moment, had been remembering the occasion when the carriage, carrying the happy Jessica and her new husband, had ploughed through the plate glass window of the general store. But now it was done. The 'Robert Whitworth' had been eased along 'Way Foot' and down the slip way and the townsfolk, who had watched in awe as the procession passed through the streets, now crowded onto the shore to see the launching. Ruth had stood with her uncle and aunt at the entrance to The Bolts and seen her husband pass by. So intent had he been on the task in hand, that he had quite failed to notice her or indeed anyone else of his acquaintance. Now she found him on the landing and went to his side.

"That was well done Daniel." she said enthusiastically.

"'T'were the horses Ruth. Couldn't have been done without our horses."

The pride was very evident in his voice and she noted that it was a pride in his animals rather than that of his own achievement. They stood together as the crew prepared to launch the boat, taking advice from the locals as to the best point of entry to the sea. Finally the lifeboat took to the water at 2:00 p.m. and pulled desperately towards the wreck, some two miles south of the landing and about one mile out to sea.

The seas were tremendous and, as the boat struggled against them, they were nearly swamped on several occasions.

Each time they were hit by a massive roller the watchers on shore held their breath until she emerged again from the foam. But then disaster struck. A tremendous wave hit the lifeboat and broke six of the oars like match wood. Two men had been knocked unconscious and the steering oar was useless so Henry Freeman had to make the terrible decision to abandon the attempt and put back to shore. The six survivors in the long boat had witnessed all and were thrown into despair at the sight of their would be saviours retreating. They had been in their open craft for over six hours exposed to the all that the elements could throw at them and their condition was deteriorating with each hour. Young Algie was unconscious and could not be roused, whilst another young apprentice had become delirious. "Don't worry lads, they'll try again." Jonathon encouraged them but without much conviction. In fact he was right and the new attempt was made more quickly than he might have hoped.

Back on shore John Storr commandeered the oars from the old Bay lifeboat which, unlike the vessel itself, were in reasonable condition. Meanwhile Henry Freeman was calling for volunteers to replace the two injured men and two more, who were simply too exhausted to go out again. There was no shortage of offers and Henry found himself with a complement of eighteen men, five more than he had had available for the first attempt. Most were local, including a Bay man who had sailed before on the 'Visiter' but there was one bearded and heavily built man who seemed to be a stranger. With the oars now double banked the 'Robert Whitworth' was re-launched and rowed vigorously towards the waiting survivors and the difficult rescue was accomplished. It was exceptionally difficult because in addition to the tumultuous seas, each man had to be lifted out of the longboat, being incapable of moving for himself. It was clear that they were all suffering from severe exposure. It was 4:00 p.m. by the time they reached the shore and safety.

Meanwhile the good people of Baytown, and most especially the womenfolk, had not stood idly by. There was going to be a need for warmth, food and clothing for both rescuers and rescued and there was an enthusiastic response to calls for help. Ruth and her aunt had naturally been a part of this co-ordination of hospitality. Rapid negotiations had taken place between the organisers of the Congregational Bazaar, which was being held that day and the landlady of the 'King's Arms' at 'Way Foot' and food supplies were pooled and taken across to the Hotel, which was made ready for the influx of people. Cheers from the shore announced the safe landing of the lifeboat and the party was escorted to the 'King's Arms' without delay. It was a bustling throng, but through the press of people Daniel caught sight of the bearded stranger, who had been part of the replacement crew, and something about him seemed familiar. Pushing his way through he crowd, he reached the man and offering his hand he said

"That was a grand thing you did; to go off with the boat and help rescue our lads. Can I maybe buy you a drink?" He peered more closely and then exclaimed "By God, its Dick isn't it? Dick Chapman? How have you been doing all these years?"

"Aye t'is me all right and ah've managed well enough, no thanks to you Daniel Robinson" was the reply. "Well, I'll shake your hand, but I'll not take a drink. Hot tea is what I crave most just now. You've done well for yourself by all accounts since I was forced to leave the district but I believe you 'ad a nasty blow in the loss of your wife and I'm sorry for it. A nice lass Miss Farlam. Better na' you deserved young Daniel." but he smiled as he said the words and Daniel was glad that time had apparently healed yet another old breach.

There was opportunity for just a few more words before Dick was snatched away by an enthusiastic lady and plied with tea and cakes. Glancing round, Daniel saw Ruth tending to the pale and still shivering Master of the 'Visiter', chafing his feet, from which the boots and sodden stockings had been removed. He tore his gaze away from her ministrations and searched for Henry Freeman to offer his congratulations. He was relieved to discover that this worthy was not at all averse to the idea of a glass of hot rum in place of the milder beverages which were on offer, so he steered him into the back parlour of the Hotel, where they could have a quiet chat and stimulating drink together. It was getting dark and Daniel raised the question of returning the lifeboat to Whitby but the cox explained that there was little point in taking her back at the present time, as it would still be impossible to negotiate the Whitby harbour entrance, with the storm still raging as it was. They would haul her up onto the slip way, make her secure and leave her until it was possible to bring her back by tugboat. At this Daniel bethought him of his horses. He wanted to make sure they had been well cared for in his absence and he said so, making his excuses to leave. "Reet, Ah'll say good day to thee then." said Harry as he rose to shake hands. There were no further words spoken but each appraised the other with that frank look of acknowledgement of his contribution to the successful operation.

Returning to the crowded main barroom and peering through the thick atmosphere, Daniel spotted Ruth doing the rounds with yet another tray of scalding hot tea. He motioned to her to join him and, handing over the tray to another woman, she did so.

"Ruth I need to get back to see to the horses. I suppose the lads will have done everything necessary but I must just make sure they are all right. I can send the trap back for you later."

He looked slightly apologetic at this admission that he might be fussing but she knew his concern was genuine.

"No need Daniel" she replied quietly. "I'll just get my shawl and come with you."

"But don't you want to stay and, well, see to – – " he trailed off into an awkward silence but nodded in the general direction of Jonathon.

"No, there's nothing here for me now. I want to be with you Daniel; I want to go home."

Steering her to the door with his arm around her shoulder he paused for a moment to bend down and kiss her.

"Th'as a grand lass Ruth." he said.